THE DUCHESS OF SYDNEY

Convicted of a crime she did not commit, and sentenced to the colonies in Australia, Georgiana had lost all hope ... until she met Francis Brooks, Lieutenant on the transport ship and tasked with protecting her. Would she ever unravel all the secrets that kept them apart, and would she ever be free again — free to be herself, and free to love?

DAWN KNOX

THE DUCHESS
OF SYDNEY

Complete and Unabridged

LINFORD
Leicester

First published in Great Britain in 2020

First Linford Edition
published 2021

A catalogue record for this book is available
from the British Library.

ISBN 978–1–4448–4759–8

Published by
Ulverscroft Limited
Anstey, Leicestershire

Printed and bound in Great Britain by
TJ Books Ltd., Padstow, Cornwall

This book is printed on acid-free paper

To Mum,
I love you forever and always

1

Georgiana gripped the rope handrail of the gangway with one hand, bracing herself against the brisk sea breeze which tugged at her cloak and threatened to blow her cap into the swell below. Ahead, the timbers of the Lady Amelia creaked and groaned as the wind buffeted the furled sails, and behind her, women cursed and moaned as they followed her up the gangplank.

She turned briefly as the figure in front of her refused to board the ship and was grabbed by two sailors who hurled her onto the deck. It gave Georgiana enough time to glance back at the English coastline and to commit it to memory. It would be many years, if ever, before she saw her homeland again.

'Move!' the seaman at the top of the gangway yelled above the wind, seizing

1

her cloak and pulling her onto the ship. He nodded at his friend and winked, 'I wouldn't mind this one,' he said and she shivered as she saw them both leer at her. The girls in the prison had told her that female convicts were often claimed by crew-members during the voyage to New South Wales, to be used as they liked.

'Name?' the officer shouted. If he'd heard the sailor's comments, or witnessed the obscene gesture he'd made when Georgiana had passed, the officer gave no sign.

She told him.

'Aylwood, G,' he shouted, ticking her off his list. He jerked his head to indicate she should follow the other women. She glanced once more towards land but much of it was now obscured by a cold, damp sea mist which had descended.

Georgiana followed the woman in front down to a lower deck. Along the length of the ship, berths were arranged in groups of four either side of a central aisle, so close together there was barely any room between them. An officer allotted places to the women and they filed through, complaining loudly at the lack of space, headroom and air in their cramped quarters. He ignored their protests, only taking action when a large woman with red hair and sturdy arms lunged at her neighbour knocking her to the floor where they writhed, punching and kicking.

The officer blew a whistle, summoning two red jacketed marines who barged past the women and grabbed the two flailing assailants, dragging them apart. Neither of the soldiers attempted to be gentle and one hauled the nearest woman away with his arm around her neck. She scrabbled at it ineffectually with her fingers. Her opponent, the red-haired aggressor was pinned to the deck as the soldier shackled her wrists behind her back.

The officer shook. his head in contempt, 'Put the pair of them in irons to cool off,' he said and continued to allocate beds to the line of women who were still pouring onto the lower deck.

'I'm that glad Mary's gone,' the tiny woman behind Georgiana whispered, 'She were bad enough in prison with her vicious temper. But I expect she'll be back afore long,' she added with a sigh, staring at the two empty berths which were waiting for the sharp-tongued red-headed woman and the girl she'd attacked. Georgiana knew what her tiny neighbour meant as she'd seen Mary Norris set upon several women and had herself once been pinned against the prison wall and threatened because her accent was *too fancy fer her own good.*

'I'm Sarah,' the tiny woman said, 'It looks like we're going to be sleeping next to each other.'

The officer called out their names and indicated their cots with the stem of his pipe. He directed a skinny woman carrying a young child to the bed next to Sarah and the woman carefully placed the girl in it. Both mother and daughter were deathly pale and in the lantern light, Georgiana could see they were

4

both sweating, Fever? Georgiana wondered. Once again, she wished the judge had not allowed himself to be persuaded to commute her death sentence to seven years transportation.

Not that she wanted to die.

She was, after all, only eighteen years old and had a yearning for life which only another person who'd been condemned to death might understand. The thought of hanging was horrific. But since she'd been in prison, she'd seen many fellow convicts killed through illness or violence. Now she was cooped up with about one hundred women, some so impervious to the threat of punishment, they'd behave in the most unpredictable and dangerous manner. Even in prison, the warders had been reluctant to deal with them unless armed. As well as the threat of violence, the current crowded conditions would make them vulnerable to diseases which would spread rapidly throughout the prison deck.

Even if she managed to survive the voyage, what would she find in New

South Wales? She'd heard about the famine and harsh conditions in the new colony of Sydney as well as the savage people who roamed across the country, spearing settlers and stealing crops.

One major fear was whether Georgiana could trust the word of her cousin, Margaret. If she could, then at least she'd be assured her ailing mother would be cared for. But her cousin wasn't the most honest of girls. After all, if it hadn't been for Margaret, Georgiana wouldn't be on this stinking prison deck, with women who behaved like animals, bound for the other side of the world.

★ ★ ★

'I didn't think it'd be so rough,' Sarah said steadying herself as the ship rolled, 'If it's going to be like this the entire voyage, I don't know how I'm going to bear it...' she tailed off and heaved.

'Lie down,' Georgiana said, helping her onto her berth, 'You'll feel better.'

She decided against telling Sarah the

sea was likely to be much rougher once they set sail in the morning and reached the open seas. When Georgiana had been a young girl, her father had read her stories about ships sailing to foreign shores, facing mountainous waves which crashed onto the decks, sweeping sailors away. On several occasions, he'd travelled to Portugal onboard a ship similar to the Lady Amelia and he'd told Georgiana that although he'd never experienced anything like what happened in those stories, there'd been a storm during which the vessel had been tossed about and he'd feared for his life. That, he told her, had been the first and only time he'd experienced sea sickness.

It seemed Georgiana had inherited his ability to resist motion sickness. Around her, women were groaning, some staggering to the buckets at the end of the deck where they heaved and vomited. At least she felt fine, although how long she'd maintain that state was doubtful in the rising temperature and oppressive atmosphere of the prison deck once the ship really started to roll.

How was she going to bear it?

Perhaps she wouldn't have to. At some point along the voyage, she might be allowed up on the top deck and if she flung herself overboard that would be an end to it. The thought comforted her. For the first time in longer than she could remember, she felt something in her life was under her control. Of course, she'd have to be allowed on deck first …

While she'd been in prison awaiting transportation, Kathleen Findlay, one of her fellow prisoners had talked about her sister, Betsy, who'd been one of the convicts shipped out to New South Wales on the Second Fleet in 1789. For the price of a tot of rum, Betsy had engaged the services of a felon who could write. He'd once been a clerk in a successful business in London who'd embezzled large sums of money from his employer to cover his debts until his double-dealing had been discovered and he'd been sentenced to death. His sentence had been shortened to transportation and now, most evenings, he could be found in one of the grog shops, penning letters for his fellow convicts. The letters were sent back to England on the infrequent ships which stopped in Sydney, often returning home via India or China.

Betsy had described being shackled to the other prisoners while on board the ship that transported her, and rarely being allowed up on deck to exercise because the ship's master was afraid of the women rioting. Many had died during the voyage and others arrived sick and weak, unable to work. Betsy complained of sores around her ankles which had persisted for months.

Finally, all the women were aboard and had been assigned a berth and most of the sailors and marines had left the prison deck except a few who loitered at the far end. They remained near the ladder, talking and laughing with some of the women. It appeared they shouldn't have been there because as soon as they heard male voices, they grabbed the steps, ready to climb up.

So far, the women hadn't been man-acled together although perhaps the ship's master might give orders for that once the women were allowed on the upper deck. Assuming, of course, that he allowed them up to take the air. If they were chained together, it would certainly prevent Georgiana from carrying out her plan.

Kathleen Findlay, sister of Betsy, was lying in the bed opposite Georgiana. She tutted and raised her eyes to the low ceiling when she caught Georgiana's eye. 'Looks like most o' them are going to make poor sailors!' she said, surveying those around her who were lying in their berths, groaning, and heaving. 'My sister, Betsy, said the worst thing about the voyage was the stink. And it'll get worse, you mark my words,' she added, 'once they starts dying.'

The sickly woman with the young girl called out, 'Water! Will someone bring me water, please!'

Georgiana climbed out of her cot and made her way to the fresh water bucket.

'I wouldn't,' Kathleen said, 'Afore you know it, you'll be down with the fever too. I'd leave them to it. Sooner they dies, the sooner there'll be more room for the rest o' us.'

'I can't listen to her cry out for water!' Georgiana was appalled.

'Well, don't say I didn't warn yer,' Kathleen said with a shrug.

'God bless you,' the sickly woman whispered when Georgiana supported her daughter's lolling head and held the cup to her lips, although the child appeared too weak to drink, and water dribbled down her chin.

'Too soft for yer own good. You won't live to see the New World,' Kathleen said as Georgiana helped the mother drink too.

At the far end of the deck, the sailors who'd been talking to the convicts hastily climbed the ladder as footsteps could be heard thudding across the deck above. Seconds later, the master and several of his officers descended to the prison deck. The ship's master was small and portly with a stomach so large his waistcoat was at bursting point. He introduced himself as Edgar Yeats in a booming voice which carried down the aisle to the far end of the deck.

'The lanterns will be removed at eight o'clock each evening and there will be no leaving this deck until morning. Your berths are arranged in groups of four and you will eat with those in your group. One woman from each group will go on deck and bring back your rations. While at sea, you will have the use of the poop and quarterdeck during the day and exercise will be allowed in clement weather. I expect you to obey my officers at all times. Misdemeanours will be treated with the utmost rigour, and if the need arises, I will have no compunction at carrying out the death penalty. Already two of your number are in irons. There they will remain until I see fit to release them. I will not tolerate brawling, nor will I countenance lewdness or immorality aboard my ship.'

Raucous laughter came from the far

end of the deck as several of the women showed their contempt for the ship's master and his demands.

Captain Yeats dabbed his nose delicately with a handkerchief and, appearing not to notice, carried on, 'Previous voyages have taken up to eleven months although we hope to make it to New South Wales in less than that, but ultimately, our journey will depend on the weather and tides. So, for those among you who do not abide by my rules, you will have ample time to repent.' He dabbed his nose again and after having a quiet word with his first mate, he turned and climbed the steps to the upper deck.

'No lewdness or immorality aboard my ship,' one of the women mimicked in a fair imitation of the master's voice. A few of the women laughed but most were too queasy to take any interest.

Once the echoes of the master's footsteps had died away; the sailors who'd been loitering at the far end of the prison deck slipped down the ladder and Georgiana saw one of them lead a woman away.

Kathleen caught Georgiana's eye, 'She'll be with child afore too long,' she remarked, 'although if she's clever, she'll have got herself a bit of protection.'

'What do you mean?'

'Betsy told me the women who took a lover were the ones who had a better time of it. Their men protected them … well, mostly. You're a pretty thing. If I was you, I'd make yerself available to one o' the officers. That way, yer might still be alive at the end o' the voyage.'

* * *

Georgiana climbed on her bed and, lying down, turned away from Kathleen and closed her eyes. It was childish to try to make the world go away by ignoring it, but she didn't know what else to do. While she'd been in prison, she'd seen a woman who'd lost her reason. One of the inmates told Georgiana the woman had been locked up for so long, she'd simply chosen to *take her mind somewheres else*.

Georgiana understood. The other women — like the red-headed, hot-tempered Mary — coped 'with life' by lashing out with their fists. Others like Kathleen either denied any emotions until they withered and died or perhaps they'd had nothing kindly about them in the first place. But Georgiana hadn't been brought up in that sort of world. She remembered being loved by her father before he'd died. Her mother loved her too, in her own way, although her health had suffered when she'd lost her husband and since that time, she'd been withdrawn, even with her daughter. Nothing had been the same since Papa had died. But at least Georgiana remembered being part of a world where people were kind and gentle.

She didn't know how to deal with this new, harsh reality. Neither did she know the rules that the women around her recognised. There seemed to be two ways for her to cope; either she put an end to everything, or she allowed her reason to ebb away until she didn't care what happened.

More women were being sick and she pulled the itchy blanket up over her face to keep out the smell. She had no idea how long she'd dozed but she awoke to hear women laughing and jeering, followed by a male voice cursing. Georgiana pulled the blanket higher, until she realised he'd called, 'Which one of yer is Georgiana Aylwood?'

'That's 'er!' Kathleen said, presumably pointing her out.

'Up!' the man said pulling the blanket off her. 'Pack yer bedding up and come with me.'

'Lucky girl! Yer caught yersel' a handsome one there and no mistake!' one of the women shouted and several of the others laughed.

Georgiana recognised the sailor as being one of the men who'd been with the ship's master earlier when he'd spoken to the convicts.

He'd have heard Captain Yeats say

he didn't allow lewdness or immorality on his ship so surely, he couldn't be doing as Kathleen had told her the officers did, and claimed a woman for his own use? But why else would he have told her to take her bedding and follow him? Georgiana shuddered. The man was taller than her and sturdily built with a large head which seemed to sprout from his broad shoulders with no sign of a neck. His bulbous nose was crooked as if he'd been involved in many fist fights and one eye was black as if the last one hadn't been long before.

'She's just a chit of a girl,' one of the women persisted, 'What you want's a real woman —'

'Well, I might just be back to take up yer kind offer,' the man said with a smile which revealed blackened teeth. He grabbed Georgiana's shoulder and propelled her along the aisle towards the ladder.

'Where are you taking me?' said Georgiana.

'Lieutenant Brooks asked to see yer. Looks like yer made an impression on 'im.'

'Who is he?' Georgiana asked in alarm.

'The government agent. Looks all right. A bit arrogant if you ask me. Fancy taking the pickings before any of the other officers 'ave 'ad a chance to look over the ladies!'

He knocked on the door of a cabin and when a voice came from inside to enter, he opened the door and jerked his head for Georgiana to proceed. She swallowed and stepped into the tiny cabin.

The officer was sitting at his desk and he looked up when she entered.

'Thank you, Griffiths,' he said, dismissing the sailor. Once the door had closed, he looked her up and down for a few seconds and slowly shook his head as if disappointed, 'So, this is Georgiana Aylwood. Well, you'd better make your bed,' he said pointing at the only berth in the cabin.

'I insist on cleanliness,' he added, 'so you'll clean yourself before you go to bed tonight and after that, you'll wash daily. I don't want this cabin overrun with vermin.'

'I always wash daily!' Georgiana said quickly, 'Well, when I'm allowed fresh water that is.'

He leaned back in his chair, crossed his ankles and surveyed her with sardonic amusement.

'I see you're spirited,' he commented, 'Yes, I can understand how that might have been a problem in prison ... but then whose fault is it when one finds oneself in such a place?'

'I've found, since I've been in such a place, that there are many reasons why a woman might find herself there. Destitution being one such reason. I don't suppose you have any idea how persuasive an empty stomach might be when there's food within reach.'

'Is that your excuse? An empty stomach? I understand you stole a watch and sundry other items to the value of eight guineas.' Georgiana hung her head. 'Nothing to say?' he asked.

'I have nothing to say to you on the matter. I am now paying for my crimes and ultimately, God will be my judge.'

'Yes, very spirited indeed ...' he said, resting his chin on his steepled fingers, then with a sigh, he added, 'Well, so long as you do as I tell you, I'm not interested in your crimes or indeed, anything else about you. I expect you to clean my cabin, fetch my meals, wash my laundry and sew if necessary. And, needless to say, to keep your hands off anything that doesn't belong to you.'

'That's all you expect?' Georgiana asked.

'Was there something I missed,' he asked, turning his head on one side as he considered. He followed her gaze to the bed. 'Ah! I see,' he said with a nod, 'Don't flatter yourself, Miss Aylwood. Your services in that area will not be required. I shall sleep on the floor. If this arrangement displeases you, I shall be quite happy to have you returned to the prison quarters. But I would think very carefully before you make such a decision ...'

Could it be true? Did this officer simply want a housekeeper? If so, she'd certainly been lucky. But why had he chosen her?

'I'd like to stay, please sir.'

'Very well.' He turned back to the letter he'd been writing when she'd arrived, 'Then make yourself busy tidying up... Oh, just one more thing,', he added as she carried her bedding to the berth, 'If anyone asks, tell them you're my sea-wife ... with all that role entails. Understand?'

* * *

Georgiana couldn't understand why Lieutenant Brooks, who'd made it clear he wanted nothing to do with her, insisted on showing her to the galley and introducing her to the cook and fellow officers on the way. It wasn't as if she couldn't have found her own way if he'd given her directions but perhaps the cook wouldn't give food to a convict unless he knew it was for an officer.

She was aware of the exchange of winks and knowing smiles between lieutenant Brooks and the other men but she kept her eyes down and pretended not to notice. It was humiliating but at least if they thought she was his 'sea wife', as he'd put it, no one would take liberties with her. Perhaps that was why he'd been at such pains to make it clear she belonged to him. Although why he should bother, she had no idea.

He left the cabin shortly after his meal and instructed her to go to bed after she'd washed his plate and cup. Georgiana climbed onto the berth and pulled the covers to her chin. Would he keep his word and sleep on the floor? She had no doubt he would. Several of the officers had eyed her with appreciation when Lieutenant Brooks had introduced her to them earlier and he'd placed a protective arm around her but as soon as they'd returned to his cabin and they were alone, he'd demonstrated complete indifference to her.

She wondered if he was married or

perhaps had a woman waiting for him in England, someone he was devoted to. But if that was so. Why was he so keen for his fellow officers to believe she was his sea-wife? It was perplexing but whatever the explanation, she was grateful because he'd rescued her from months of hardship on the prison deck. In effect, he had saved her life because there was now no need to consider the possibility of hurling herself into the sea and ending it all. She'd do whatever was necessary to remain under his protection throughout the voyage. Then once she reached New South Wales, she'd reassess her position, although it heartened her to think that if she could survive this journey, perhaps she could face the new colony with courage.

So, how far would she be prepared to go, to remain under lieutenant Brooks' protection? She weighed the advantages and disadvantages, as her father had taught her to do years ago. Having the freedom of most of the ship and sharing a cabin with a man who appeared to hold her in contempt was far preferable to being confined to a restricted area and sleeping with a hundred other women, some of whom were sick, unpredictable or dangerous. She could almost hear her father telling her to react appropriately depending on the prevailing conditions.

But how would her mother advise her? Georgiana knew her guidance would be based on morality and social expectations. In Mama's genteel world, respectable women would never choose to spend time alone with a strange man, much less sleep in the same room. If Georgiana had been faced with this decision many months before her arrest, she'd have known what to do. The pressure to conform to society's rules would have been overwhelming and any deviation from expected behaviour would have provoked condemnation from everyone in her social circle. But before she'd been arrested, this dilemma would never have arisen. And now? How should she behave? She suspected the advice Papa would have given her would be the best to heed. React appropriately upon prevailing conditions.

Not that it mattered because if the officer changed his mind, there would be nothing she could do about it anyway. But it mattered to her whether, in her mind, she accepted it or not. He would never know, of course. And if he did know, he probably wouldn't care. But she would know that if she'd had the power to decide, she would have chosen to allow him such freedom or not.

So, the question appeared to be, was the relative comfort the lieutenant was offering worth the loss of her virginity? In society's eyes, she was a felon, a shameful woman being removed from her homeland to the furthest reaches imaginable, along with fallen women who were used to selling their bodies for paltry sums and others who had no misgivings about burgling, stealing and defrauding. There were no prospects of Georgiana making a suitable match. The chance of her marrying at all was slight. Who would care if it was assumed she was selling herself?

No one. Because the truth was, no one cared about her at all. So, it was up to her to make up the rules as she saw fit.

Her thoughts were interrupted when she heard the latch lift slowly and the door open. She held her breath. Suppose it wasn't Lieutenant Brooks? But she recognised his silhouette against the lantern light outside. The smell of rum wafted into the cabin and she could tell by his exaggerated movements that he'd been drinking. Would he forget she was in his bed and climb in?

He'd obviously forgotten she was there because he tripped over the pallet he'd told her to make up for him on the floor and dropped the shoes he'd been carrying with a clatter. She could hear him grunting at the effort of undressing but finally, he lay down and shortly after, his breath, deep and regular could be heard.

Georgiana settled down to sleep. The Lady Amelia would weigh anchor at six o'clock the following morning — or more accurately, that morning, since Lieutenant Brooks had not returned until well after midnight. In a few hours, the voyage to the other side of the world would begin in earnest. If their destination had been the furthest reaches of the universe, it could hardly have seemed more distant.

★ ★ ★

When Georgiana finally woke, Lieutenant Brooks had risen, dressed and left. She was amazed she'd slept for so long but, she reminded herself, it was the first uninterrupted sleep she'd had since she'd been arrested and imprisoned. She washed and dressed quickly and after tidying away the lieutenant's bed, she hurried to the galley to fetch his meal.

She had no way of knowing if he'd already eaten but surely if he had, an extra bowl of burgoo — oatmeal porridge sweetened with molasses — would be welcome.

By the time he returned to the cabin, she was busy sewing a button on his coat which had been hanging by a thread. The cries of the sailors, the motion and flapping of the sails and creaking of the timbers told her they'd set sail.

Lieutenant Brooks greeted her politely and nodded, as if in approval, when he noticed the breakfast and her efforts to mend his coat.

'I'll be back to eat at midday. You're permitted on deck but keep out of everyone's way. For the next three or four hours, the Isle of Wight should be visible. Perhaps that might interest you. After that, there'll be precious little to see until we reach Tenerife.' He nodded politely and left.

How wonderful it was to roam freely, especially on deck where the crisp, salty wind blew away the smell of the prison and from time to time, whipped up spray which soaked her face and hair. The convicts were brought up to an area on deck which had been separated off, presumably to keep the women from distracting the men and keep the men away from the women. Sarah waved to Georgiana although Kathleen turned away and made no sign she'd seen her.

From the elevated position of the poop-deck, Edgar Yeats and lieutenant Brooks looked down on the milling convicts on the quarterdeck. The two men were deep in conversation and eventually, they went below together, the master with his hands clasped behind his back pushing his stomach even further forward.

At midday when Georgiana took the lieutenant's meal to the cabin she found him writing at his desk. He tapped the desktop to indicate where she should place the platter and cup and she silently laid them down.

'I've had your chest brought up from the hold,' he said without looking up, 'I thought you might prefer to wear your own clothes.'

She looked down at her shabby, striped prison jacket and skirt.

'Thank you!' That was the last thing

she'd expected. Kathleen had said her sister, Betsy, had written to tell her that on one of the ships of the Second Fleet, the master had ordered the convicts' chests and boxes to be flung overboard

'I won't require a meal this evening. I'm dining with Captain Yeats and several of the passengers,' he said, watching her obvious delight at finding her books, 'If you find reading pleasurable, I'd be happy to lend you some of my books, although, of course they may not be to your taste.'

Georgiana went to fetch her meal from the coppers on deck where the convicts' meals were prepared and by the time she returned to the cabin, Lieutenant Brooks was changing. He appeared annoyed when she entered but his expression changed to relief when he saw her.

'I've caught my signet ring,' he said, holding up an arm to show her how it had snagged on his cuff. She gently untangled the lace from the bezel and freed the ring. He took it from his finger and continued dressing.

'Would you like me to sew this now?' she asked, frowning at the tear in the lace.

'No, I don't want to arrive late. Perhaps you can mend it tomorrow.'

She nodded, 'Yes, of course. Do you want me to leave until you've finished dressing?"

'No.' He sounded surprised, 'I don't suppose I'm the first man you've seen dressing.'

'Well, you suppose incorrectly!' she snapped, 'That is quite a presumption to make!'

'If you say so,' he said with a hint of a smile, 'Am I to believe you're the only female convict who wouldn't sell her body for a farthing?'

'I have no interest in your beliefs. Neither am I an expert about female convicts. I can only speak for myself. I have never seen a man undress and ...' She was about to say that neither would she sell her body for gain when she remembered her decision the previous evening to do whatever it took to maintain her position as his nominal sea-wife. ' ... and neither would I sell my body for money.' That at least was true.

He smiled and held out his jacket for her to take, 'Well, even a completely innocent girl such as yourself must surely have seen a man put on a jacket, perhaps you'd help me with mine.'

He turned and slipped his arms in the sleeves of the jacket she held out for him, then straightened the lace at his cuffs and neck.

'Am I passable?' he asked with a glimmer of a smile, pretending to preen in a mirror.

'I'm sure you have no interest in the opinion of a mere convict,' she said, laughing at his foolishness, despite the hurt she'd felt at his opinion of her.

After he'd gone, she realised he'd forgotten to put his signet ring back on and fearing he'd throw his clothes over it when he returned, like he had the previous evening, and perhaps knocking it on the floor, she put the ring in the box on his desk in which he kept his quills.

Once he'd gone, she read for a while until her eyes tired in the dim lantern-light, then blowing out the candle, she went to bed. What would the dinner party in the master's cabin be like? Periodically, she heard the braying laugh of Mrs Leston, wife of Reverend Andrew Leston, the minister. The couple were paying their way to New South Wales where they planned to serve the ungodly of Sydney. As such, they were guests on the Lady Amelia. Georgiana had seen them earlier walking on the deck, observing the convicts they intended to save with distaste on their faces and much shaking of heads in pious consternation. She wondered whether Lieutenant Brooks had divulged to the master and his guests that he'd taken a sea-wife for the duration of the voyage.

She woke some time later when Lieutenant Brooks quietly opened the door and slipped in. Unlike the previous evening, she wasn't alarmed at his reappearance. He'd shown very little interest in her at all and there was no indication that was likely to change. The rustling of his clothes told her he was undressing in the darkness and the sound of tearing suggested he'd caught the ripped lace and had torn it further. He swore softly and there was silence for a few moments, followed by the sound of sliding books across the desk top.

She could tell through her closed eyelids he'd lit the lantern and opening them a fraction, she could see him piling up his account books and journal. Turning abruptly, he strode to her bed, holding the lantern aloft and seized her wrist, then held the light near it. Georgiana squealed in alarm and bringing her other hand out from beneath the blankets, she tried to fend him off but he grabbed that hand and held it to the light.

'Where's my ring?' he demanded.

'I ... I ... in the box.'

He dropped, her hand and strode to her chest, then raising the lid, he pulled her clothes out and dumped them on the floor. Holding the lantern so it illuminated the interior of the chest, he peered into the bottom.

She was fully awake now, 'Not my chest! Your box. The one where you keep your quills!'

He stopped and rising to his feet, he moved to the desk.

'It's in the front, right hand corner,' she added.

He fished in the box and by the light of the lamp, she saw him slip the ring on his finger. Still, he remained silent until with, a sigh, he turned to her and said, 'I humbly beg your pardon, madam.'

'Granted,' she said curtly. She sat up in bed and pulled the blankets to her chin, 'I can see how you might conclude I'd stolen it. After all, I am a convicted criminal. I can even see how you might expect me to steal it. What I am struggling to understand, is why you want me here in your cabin at all. You neither like me nor trust me. I cannot comprehend why you want me here.'

'Well, if you must know, looking after

you was a condition of being given this appointment.'

She stared at him, her eyes wide in disbelief. 'Who ...' she asked with a shake of her head, 'Who would have demanded that of you?'

'Your Uncle Thomas.'

'Uncle Thomas? Judge Thomas Tilcott?'

Georgiana asked incredulously, 'He asked you to look after me? But why?'

'I've been wondering that myself. But he didn't elaborate. He simply told me to make sure I can even see how you arrived safely in Sydney. I've no idea what he thinks might happen after your arrival. Once the Lady Amelia discharges her cargo in Sydney Cove, my obligation is concluded because we'll be leaving for China shortly after loading supplies.'

'And this position means so much to you that you agreed?'

'Yes,' he said firmly, 'Yes, it did. Thomas and I are related and he has some influence in the government, so he recommended me as agent of the Crown to sail with the Lady Amelia. It was too good an opportunity to refuse.'

'Even if it meant you had to look after a convict?'

'If you're part of Thomas' family, then we're related — albeit distantly and by marriage. And yes, if that was the price to pay ..."

'So, we know where we stand. You offer me protection and in return, I clean, fetch meals, sew and resist stealing your personal items,' she said with a bitter laugh.

'I've offered my apologies for the mistake. But under the circumstances, it was a reasonable assumption to make.'

'I'm not sure whether to be more insulted at your suspicions that I'd stolen your ring or at your belief that I'd be so stupid as to take it and attempt to keep that fact from you for the next few months! If I were dishonest and I had stolen your ring, I assure you, I'd have found a far more inaccessible place than my own finger!'

'If I were dishonest,' he said in mocking tones, 'Fine words from a convicted felon! Thomas warned me about you. Sadly, I didn't listen. I took you at face value but thank you for the warning. I shall lock everything away in future.'

'I may be a convicted felon but I swear before God I am not dishonest!'

'How can that be? You were tried and convicted. Thomas told me you confessed to the crimes.'

'If you were anyone other than a relative of Uncle Thomas, I might in time have explained. But now, I cannot.' She lay down and turned away from him, not wanting him to see the hot, stinging tears which slid between her eyelids. It shouldn't have mattered what his opinion was of her because in several months' time, she would once again be on her own, working with the other convicts in Sydney. But since he'd removed her from the prison, he was now the only person who didn't eye her with suspicion and distaste or with lust and contempt. Being distantly related should have forged a bond between them. But now, he'd be more interested in how much distance there was between them, wanting to be as far as possible from the criminal element of the family. And she couldn't tell him anything about her life and risk him finding out about Margaret. Mama's wellbeing and happiness depended on that.

2

Lieutenant Francis Brooks lay for some time listening to the creaking of the ship and the howl of the wind in the sails and rigging. Shortly after he'd doused the light, he'd heard what sounded like a sob from the girl, but he couldn't be sure. That had surprised him because after Thomas had warned him she was dishonest and deceitful, it seemed strange she hadn't tried to gain his sympathy by sobbing hysterically. He had no doubt she'd been crying since her eyes had brimmed before she'd turned away.

Too late, he remembered Thomas had warned him not to tell the girl about their connection nor about their arrangement. The wine and port at Captain Yeats' table had been remarkably good and the master had been generous to his guests which resulted in Francis drinking more than he'd intended. Although he'd vowed to cut down, he'd definitely drunk too much and spoken before thinking. Something else he'd vowed to stop.

Georgiana Aylwood was an enigma. She wasn't what he'd expected at all and he was pleasantly surprised because she had dignity, unlike the other convicts. Her spirit marked her out. It wasn't the brazen boldness of many of the prisoners who claimed to be innocent, despite incontrovertible evidence to the contrary. No, strangely, Georgiana had even confessed to her crimes. For such a seemingly intelligent woman, that had been remarkably stupid ... or perhaps exceedingly clever. Unlike the other convicts, she would most likely win people's trust. And when a criminal had their victim's trust, anything was possible — fraud, blackmail — and recently, Francis had been anything but discreet. Was that why Thomas had warned him about her?

When Francis had received an invitation to dine with Thomas, his life had been one of excess — brandy, gambling and women, although his career in the Royal Navy hadn't started like that, he'd merely tried to keep abreast of his fellow naval officers. Unfortunately for Francis, most of them had fortunes at their disposal to bail them out when the cards were unfavourable, or influential families to smooth over any regrettable behaviour. The Brooks family had been wealthy but Francis' portion had not been great — perhaps his father had recognised his son's rakish tendencies and had limited his allowance accordingly.

With enormous bills to pay and being pursued by several women to whom he'd made rash promises, he needed help to lift himself out of the mire. Thomas' letter arrived at exactly the right time, offering Francis an escape.

Thomas didn't fully explain his interest in the girl. He told Francis she'd admitted stealing a gold pocket watch and other items to the value of eight guineas, well over the capital punishment threshold. Accordingly, she'd been sentenced to death. However, Thomas had asked his friend, the presiding judge, to reduce her sentence to seven years transportation to New South Wales. His request had been granted and now Georgiana was on her way to the other side of the world.

Why, Francis had asked, had Thomas taken an interest in the girl? She was a distant part of his family, Thomas explained with a dismissive wave of his hand, implying great distance. And it was his Christian duty to ensure she was protected while on the voyage. There'd been outcry over the notorious Second Fleet which arrived in Sydney in 1790. Three of the ships had been contracted from a company which had previously transported slaves to North Africa and it had been important to maintain the slaves' health so they'd bring a good price on reaching their destination. However, the convicts' welfare was not critical as the company was paid a fee of £17 7s. 6d, for transportation, clothing and food for each convict, regardless of whether they lived or died. The poor conditions aboard the vessels, and the cruelty and mistreatment, had resulted in an extremely high death rate despite the presence on the fleet of a Government Agent who'd been appointed to monitor the captain and crew. On arrival in Sydney, many of the survivors were disabled or sick and a large number died.

Thomas explained he could use his influence to ensure Francis was appointed as Government Agent and in return, Francis could keep an eye on their kinswoman. Francis had been unable to believe his luck when in addition to the offer of an appointment, Thomas had paid his gambling debts. By the time Francis returned from his voyage, everyone would have forgotten about his misdemeanours and he could start anew. He'd gladly accepted the offer although looking after the girl would likely cause problems for him but apparently, Edgar Yeats was aware that his naval agent was going to take one of the women under his wing as a special favour to Thomas Tilcott.

★ ★ ★

Three weeks after she set sail from Portsmouth, the Lady Amelia arrived in Santa Cruz, capital of Tenerife. The master had intended to allow the prisoners to disembark with an escort of marines, but he changed his mind when a fight broke out between hot-tempered Mary Norris and a group of women who'd decided to teach her a lesson. Mary and three others were put in irons and the other convicts were denied access to the city.

Georgiana was disappointed. Santa Cruz looked like places her father had described during his travels across Portugal, Italy and Spain.

She'd hardly seen Lieutenant Brooks after he'd told her about his arrangement with Uncle Thomas. He appeared to be taking his post as naval agent seriously and when she'd gone to the top deck to air their bedding in the nets or queued for his meals, Georgiana often saw him walking alongside the master and the surgeon of the Lady Amelia, Joseph Dawson. From the little Francis had said, she knew he was taking the welfare of the convicts seriously and was keen to check supplies before they were loaded in Santa Cruz ready for the next leg of the journey across the Atlantic Ocean to Brazil.

Francis had told her that the master and the surgeon held similar opinions to him and that if they could stave off scurvy and other illnesses which plagued ships at sea, he was hopeful most of the convicts would arrive safely. The sickly woman and her daughter had both been buried at sea a week after leaving England but luckily, if they'd died of a disease, it hadn't spread.

On arriving in Santa Cruz, the master, Lieutenant Brooks and several of the ship's officers were invited to dine with the governor of the Canary Islands and each evening after that, Georgiana knew that many of the officers went ashore, sampling the delights of the town. Lieutenant Brooks, however, spent his time working onboard.

The weather had turned much warmer and the cabin was stifling despite the open windows, so she often slept in her shift on top of the blankets, trying to cool down. Sails had been rigged over the hatches to increase the ventilation to the prison deck, but she couldn't imagine the temperatures the convicts were enduring. Lieutenant Brooks often didn't return to the cabin and she assumed he was sleeping on deck or perhaps working with the master until the early hours.

However, on their last night in port, he dressed formally and told her he'd been invited once again to dine with the governor in his residence and would return late. The stores of food, water and wine had been replenished and they would set sail in the morning.

Georgiana stood on the deck, watching the officers row to the shore for their final evening celebrations. For the first time since they'd arrived, the cloud had drifted away allowing a view of the mountain top bathed in the golden light of the setting sun. The white buildings of the town shone and she sighed as she heard the distant peal of bells in the church towers.

'If yer lonely, I'd be 'appy to spend some time with yer'

She hadn't heard the sailor approach and now, as he advanced towards her, she recoiled at the smell of his breath. 'Lieutenant Brooks will be back soon,' she said, dodging out of his way.

'Don't be like that,' he said in wheedling tones and, moving surprisingly quickly for such a bulky man, he blocked her way, ''E won't be back fer hours. We've time to get to know each other.'

'If you don't get out of my way, I shall tell the lieutenant on his return and he'll see you flogged!' She realised her voice was rising in panic. Many of the officers were on shore and although there were other sailors working on deck, they were ignoring what was going on.

'You don't think 'e's going to be bothered about you 'aving a bit of fun while 'e's out doing the same. The ladies of the island are very friendly.' He laughed and the blast of evil-smelling breath made her flinch.

'Turn from me, would you?' he snarled

and hit her across the cheek, 'Well. Lieutenant Brooks won't be around much longer. As soon as we dock in Sydney, 'e'll be off to China. But me ... I'm gonna make me a new life in Sydney. So, we'll be neighbours. And neighbours should be friendly to each other.' He smiled and turned to go, then called over his shoulder, 'I'll see you in Sydney.'

* * *

Georgiana slept fitfully that night in the hot, airless cabin, jumping at each unfamiliar sound, afraid the sailor would know she was alone.

She was awake at first light when the crew began to hoist the sails and after tidying the cabin, she went to the galley to fetch breakfast for Lieutenant Brooks, keeping an eye out for the sailor who'd been so persistent the previous evening. Her cheek was red but there was no black eye or bruising and she decided against telling the lieutenant. As the sailor had said, when the Lady Amelia sailed for

China, her protector would be gone. If she reported him now for his behaviour, he'd probably be flogged, and he looked like a man to bear a grudge. There was, of course, always the possibility that after she'd rejected him, he'd found another woman to pester.

On her return to the cabin, Lieutenant Brooks was at his desk. 'There's something for you on the bed,' he said without looking up, 'It's going to get hotter from now on, so you might need it.'

On the blanket was a long, thin parcel wrapped in a silk neckerchief and blue ribbon. She gently untied it to find a lacquered fan with lacy trim and silk tassels. 'For me?' she asked in amazement.

'One of my fellow officers remarked I hadn't yet bought you a gift and lectured me on the art of pleasing a woman. He purchased a fan for his wife, so I got you the same. It's best to keep up the pretence.'

'Thank you,' she said, although never had such a beautiful gift held less meaning nor given less pleasure. But he didn't reply. He'd already picked up his spoon and was eating while reading the notes he'd just written.

* * *

Francis insisted she took the fan with her when they walked on deck together but despite knowing he'd only bought it because of another man's suggestion, she was glad of it because the temperature increased daily as they headed towards the Equator and if it didn't cool her down, at least it agitated the heavy, humid air.

The weather alternated between intense heat and violent storms and even worse, they were becalmed for two days without a breath of wind.

The bloody flux broke out in the prison deck and lieutenant Brooks spent much time with Surgeon Dawson discussing how best to contain the disease. The surgeon immediately isolated the victims, placing them in his hospital and recommended the next time the weather allowed, the convicts be brought to the upper deck and the prison quarters cleaned with liberal amounts of antiseptic oil of tar. The precautions appeared to work because no one else caught the fever and those who'd succumbed, gradually recovered.

Almost three weeks after leaving Santa Cruz, the Lady Amelia was due to cross the Equator at about midday. There was an air of excitement which Georgiana noticed when she went to the galley to collect the lieutenant's pease porridge. It was as if everyone was sharing a secret except her, even Lieutenant Brooks seemed in good humour.

At mid-morning, as sailors on the upper deck began shouting and laughing, the lieutenant rushed into the cabin and beckoned for her to follow. The convicts were assembled on deck with crowds of sailors and marines who stood in groups shouting and jeering.

'What's happening?' Georgiana asked as someone began playing the bagpipes.

'Over there!' Francis pointed out the

bosun, George Clark, who was emerging from the crowd, followed by able seaman, John Wheeler, both of whom were dripping with water. George wore a loin cloth, a long, false beard and a crown on top of a wig made from rope strands. In his hand, he carried a trident which he waved about to the delight of the crowd. John was dressed in women's clothes with a neckerchief tied to hide his hair and beard. He also wore a crown.

George jumped onto a large crate and with his huge fists resting on his hips, he surveyed the crowd with mock severity, 'I am King Neptune, arisen from the ocean! And this, my lady wife, Queen Amphitrite. Or as I call her, Mrs Neptune.' The crowd whistled and roared as George heaved John, who was hampered by his skirts, onto the crate. 'Bow before me, subjects!' He swiped at the sailors who'd gathered around the crate, with his trident. 'I've risen from the sea to chastise and initiate those who've never crossed the Line before. Bring them before me for sentencing!'

A dozen blindfolded sailors. were brought forward and George interrogated each in turn, sentencing them to give up their rum ration for a week or be ducked in a large pool of sea water on the main deck. One by one, the blindfolded sailors were thrown in the pool and ducked before being allowed to clamber out and celebrate with extra rations of rum. Finally, King Neptune announced that all hands had been initiated into the rights and privileges owing to his subjects and that the ceremony had drawn to a close, but at a nod from the ship's master, the crew carried on celebrating through the afternoon and into the night. Several of the seamen brought out musical instruments and when the master allowed the convicts the freedom to dance with his men, Lieutenant Brooks took Georgiana's hand and led her into the twirling throng.

★ ★ ★

Restrictions set in place to keep the women and men apart during the voyage had been rigorously upheld although when the ship's master had ordered a surprise roll call one evening, several convicts had been found in the crew's quarters and it was reasonable to assume it wasn't the first time that women and sailors had found a way to circumvent the rules.

However, the Crossing the Line ceremony had unleashed an excitement and wildness in everyone. It was as if those who were destined to remain in Sydney permanently, both convicts and settlers, suspected life was about to become extremely challenging and they welcomed the opportunity to forget the future. English newspapers had reported that Sydney was not yet self-sufficient and despite great efforts, its people still depended on supplies from home. So, anyone who'd soon be part of the developing community knew that exhausting work and hardship lay ahead.

A lively reel began and Lieutenant Brooks and Georgiana broke away from the dancers to catch their breath.

'I can't believe Captain Yeats is being so lenient,' Francis said. With a nod of his head, he pointed out yet another couple who were slipping away, hand in hand, presumably to find a quieter part of the ship.

'It's only one evening,' she said, 'and everyone is so happy.'

'It only takes one evening,' he said with a laugh, 'Well, I suppose Captain Yeats has calculated that the Lady Amelia will be on its way to China by the time the consequences of tonight's couplings are obvious.'

The afternoon had been so full of surprise and excitement, Georgiana had forgotten the previous night's unpleasantness but now, having been reminded of Sydney and what was likely to happen after the ship had sailed, a chill of fear ran through her. She scanned the crowds for the dreadful man with the bad breath.

'You really must try harder than that,' Lieutenant Brooks said. 'If you appear so unhappy in my company, people may wonder why I choose to keep you with me.'

'Oh, yes, I'm sorry... it wasn't you. I... I was just remembering... something.'

'I see. Well, perhaps if you try a little harder to appear content in my company, it might benefit you,' he said reproachfully.

She hadn't meant to say it but the words escaped before she could stop them, 'But only while we're on board. When we reach Sydney, I'll be on my own ... I'll just be Lieutenant Brooks' discarded sea-wife!'

'Shh!' He stiffened and grabbing her arm, he led her away from the revelling crowds to the shadows further along the deck.

'Don't make it look as though we're arguing — we must appear to be devoted to each other. No one will interfere with you while you're under my protection. And yes, I understand your fears and I've already considered them. When we arrive, I'll request an audience with Sydney's governor and ask if he'll make special provision for you.'

If only it were true that no one would

interfere with her while she was under his protection! But admittedly, the sailor might have been more persistent if he hadn't feared what an officer might do. However, she was relieved that Lieutenant Brooks was genuinely concerned about her welfare, and after all, it wasn't his fault she'd be alone and defenceless once she was in Sydney.

Neither was it her fault, of course, but as she'd discovered in life, those who were most to blame were often not the ones who were punished.

'So, does that allay your fears?' he asked.

It didn't. Why would the governor treat her any differently to other convicts? But she smiled and thanked him, implying it had eased her mind. If she told him what she was afraid of, he would insist on taking action against the sailor.

'Good! Now, let's enjoy the evening! There won't be another like this. Come!' His eyes sparkled as he drew her towards the edge of the ship and with both hands on the gunwale, he leaned over to stare into the ocean, then gestured for her to do the same.

She leaned over and gasped in amazement, 'The water's glowing! How can light be coming from beneath the surface? That isn't possible!'

He laughed at her astonishment, 'I don't know what causes it. Someone once told me it comes from tiny animals in the sea but I don't know for certain. I've seen it several times before and it's usually in tropical waters like we are now.'

'It's beautiful! How wonderful it would be to scoop up armfuls of it!' Georgiana leaned further over the gunwale, her arms outstretched as if to do just that. Multi-hued, blue light glowed and sparkled beneath the surface of the inky sea. On other nights, the water had been dark with wave tops picked out in silver when the moon shone across its surface. But now the sea was vivid blue, turquoise and green and it shimmered with the movement of the ocean. She held her cap on with one hand and with the wind in her face, she looked towards the bow of the ship ploughing through the waves, throwing brightly-lit droplets of spray into the air like emeralds and sapphires. Turning to the stern, she saw the frothy wake glowing and a luminescent trail which stretched behind them, fading away, towards the horizon.

'I can't believe what's right in front of my eyes!' she said, her voice choked with the emotion of witnessing such an awe-inspiring sight, 'I've never seen anything so wondrous!'

If it hadn't been for the strains of the bagpipes and the shouts of those carousing further along the deck, she could almost have believed the Lady Amelia had slipped out of the natural world and into a magic realm where it was gliding through utter darkness over a carpet of glowing jewels.

'Look!' He stepped towards her, placing his arm around her shoulders and pointing out a shoal of fish whose gem-encrusted bodies sliced through the water. They darted alongside the ship, leaping above the surface as they chased each other and disappeared into the distance in a blue, shimmering haze. Once they'd gone, Francis remained where he was, his arm around her shoulders and his body close to hers. She felt his breath on her ear and the sensation sent shivers of delight rippling through her.

'Are you cold?' he asked, wrapping his arms around her and placing his cheek against hers.

'Just a little,' she lied, hoping he'd continue to hold her. Was it so wrong to imagine they were really sharing their lives in the way other people assumed? She knew that the morning would bring reality sharply into focus. No, she decided, it wasn't wrong at all. If she was allowed to have one enchanted night in the arms of this handsome man and to pretend they were lovers with a promising future, then tomorrow, she would willingly accept that they were merely distantly related strangers linked by a mutual relative. She told herself she would regret nothing.

'There you are, Francis! I've been looking for you everywhere!' It was Midshipman Harris who'd obviously drunk much of the brandy that was in the jug he was waving, 'Where'sh your cup? Come on, man, drink up!'

'It looks like you've had enough for both of us, Robert!' Lieutenant Brooks said.

'You can't have too much brandy. Come on man! Let'sh have a toasht!' He staggered sideways, recovered his balance and leaning against the mast, he raised the jug and his cup.

'Thank you for your offer but I have other plans, Robert ...' He winked and tilting Georgiana's face up, he placed his lips against hers. Then taking her hand, he led her away.

'Ho! I'll drink to that!' Midshipman Harris shouted and drank deeply from the jug, 'I'm going to find myself a bit o' company.'

Lieutenant Brooks put his arm around Georgiana protectively as they pushed through the rowdy crowd and made their way down to the lower deck, laughing conspiratorially. As he pulled her into the cabin, he knocked a book off his desk and in an instant, everything changed. He dropped her hand, stooped to retrieve the book and in cold tones, told her to go to bed.

The enchantment was over.

Yet the speed at which he reverted to normal shocked her. The lieutenant had been so tender on deck and although she'd known he was putting on a performance, when they'd watched the shoal of glittering, blue fish, there'd been no one else there to see what they were doing and she'd wondered... well, perhaps it might be fairer to say, she'd hoped that he hadn't been pretending.

Well, more fool her! Surely by now she'd learned that wherever she looked for happiness, misery always found her and claimed her first.

Lieutenant Brooks blew out the candle and began to remove his shirt. Usually, he left the cabin and allowed her time to undress and climb into bed before he returned but now, by the time he'd lain down, Georgiana had only removed her petticoats and was struggling with the laces of her bodice in the dark. Finally, she'd undressed to her shift and lay down too. She was wide awake and she knew from the sound of his breathing that Lieutenant Brooks was too.

★ ★ ★

Francis acknowledged with dismay that once again, he'd failed to restrain his hedonistic tendencies. He'd thrown himself into the celebrations and before he'd realised, he'd drunk too much. Thankfully, Midshipman Harris had brought him to his senses despite the fact he'd been plying him with more drink.

Francis had somehow found himself on a quiet part of deck holding Georgiana, his body pressed closely to hers, his arms wrapped around her, breathing in her delicious scent. He remembered raising his hand to turn her face towards him, and leaning in to kiss her when

Robert had burst onto the scene.

Thankfully, the shock of someone appearing in what was about to become an intimate moment, brought Francis to his senses and he'd resisted Robert Harris' offer of more brandy. At least he hadn't consumed so much he'd lost the ability to judge when to stop. Nevertheless, he'd behaved foolishly and rashly with Georgiana.

But would one kiss have been so bad?

Francis was torn. On one hand, he had a job to do. So far, he'd impressed Captain Yeats with his diligence and he knew he could make a difference to the welfare of the convicts and crew. When he returned to England, his mistakes would have been forgotten and he'd be able to afford to settle down or find another ship and sail off into uncharted waters. He'd been given this unbelievable opportunity by Thomas Tilcott and now he had to keep his side of the bargain and take care of Georgiana. He was happy to do that but the more time he spent with her, the more she attracted him.

Yet Thomas had warned him about her dishonesty. Whereas he trusted Thomas, he didn't have faith in himself. His own instincts had led him astray so often in the past because he'd been too interested in pleasure. He'd fallen for unsuitable women, and spent too much time with the sort of 'friends' who were happy to relieve him of large sums of money at the gambling table. It wasn't even as if his excesses had brought him happiness. No, he'd sworn to leave all that irresponsibility behind.

Thomas set an example to follow. He was a successful man, a family man, wise and knowledgeable. So he must be right about Georgiana ... and yet, it was impossible to believe.

He cast his mind back over the evening. He and Georgiana had joined in many of the reels and jigs until they'd walked further down the deck away from the crowd. Until that time, there hadn't been much opportunity to drink large quantities of brandy, so perhaps he hadn't had as much as he'd thought. After all, he felt quite sober. The heady euphoria he'd experienced earlier that evening had now completely disappeared. It had started when he showed Georgiana the mysterious green glow and it had increased with each moment he'd been with her. Was it possible his exhilaration hadn't been liquor-induced after all? Perhaps it had more to do with Georgiana — the feel of her body against his, the smell of attar of roses in her hair, the glimpse of rounded breasts when her neckerchief came untucked from her bodice and when he'd wrapped his arms around her, the wildly beating heart that he could feel which matched the rhythm of his own. But he'd been with her on many occasions and not reacted so rashly. What had been different? Perhaps the mysterious blue glow and the romantic atmosphere had bewitched them both.

He'd been tempted to follow his instincts and make love to her when they reached his cabin — she appeared be willing — but the reminder of his books stacked on the desk had drawn him up short. They represented his current position and his future and reminded him he'd vowed to dedicate himself to his job and to regaining his self-respect. This was his last chance and only a fool would throw it away.

Thomas had warned him against trusting Georgiana. He now wondered if perhaps it hadn't been the night which had bewitched him but the woman herself.

★ ★ ★

When Georgiana woke in the morning, the lieutenant had already left the cabin. His bedding was neatly stacked with a note on his desk to say he'd be back later than usual for breakfast. She lay there, turning over the previous night's events in her mind. Despite appearing to be sincere, he'd simply been acting a part. Of course, she'd known the new day would re-establish normality but it had happened so quickly. One minute they'd been hand in hand, hastening to his cabin and the next, he'd turned his back on her.

Now, she relived the time they'd been together, remembering every detail. If only she could capture it and carry it with her forever. A keepsake that she'd get out from time to time, to brighten what was likely to be a dreadful ordeal when they arrived in Sydney.

Last night her senses had tingled with awareness; surely such intensity, would make it easier to commit to memory? But unless she had something tangible to remind her, eventually the memories would fade.

She climbed out of bed and opening her chest, she pushed her hand to the bottom corner. When she'd located the miniature of her father, she placed it in the palm of her hand and held it to her lips. It was something like this she wished she could carry with her to remind her of the previous night. She gently stroked the frame, not wanting to touch the painting and risk damaging it, for other than a few of his books, she had nothing else that had once belonged to him.

There was no need to hurry because Lieutenant Brooks wouldn't be back for hours, so she took her time dressing and then sat on the bed, gazing at the picture of her father. It was precious because it showed him as she remembered; his face handsome and his eyes alight with laughter as if he was sharing a joke with someone. But it was also poignant because it had set the family on a disastrous course — her father dying shortly after and her mother's health failing. It wasn't quite true to say all the problems began after the painting of her father had been finished. They'd actually started after her miniature had been completed. The artist, Gianfranco Mascio, had been a friend of Papa's and he'd been engaged to paint Papa, Mama and seven-year old Georgiana.

Papa had met Gianfranco in Venice during one of his journeys around Europe and they'd kept in touch on their return. They lived within a few miles of each other in London, although the Aylwood's elegant house was situated in a fashionable area whereas the artist's rooms were across the Thames in a less salubrious parish. Papa had introduced Giarifranco to his wealthy friends, resulting in commissions to paint portraits, family groups, two race horses and even a mistress.

Georgiana had liked Gianfranco. He'd visited regularly for as long as she could remember and he'd always crouched when he spoke to her in his thick Italian accent, so they were eye-to-eye, and produced coins from her ear, making them disappear, only to reappear in her other ear. He spoke in loud, enthusiastic tones with many expansive gestures and Georgiana found him friendlier than her father's other acquaintances. Papa's scientific friends frequently visited the house but most of them ignored her. Papa bought a magnificent telescope which they spent nights peering through and against Mama's wishes, one night, when none of his friends were there,

71

Papa allowed Georgiana to stay up late and gaze at the stars with him. Her mother had not been happy, not only because it kept their daughter up late, she'd complained at the cost of such an expensive piece of equipment, the bill for which had arrived shortly after Papa announced he was off to Vienna to speak at a scientific gathering.

'This spending has to stop, Joshua! You'll make paupers of us all!' Mama had said waving her book of accounts at him but he'd simply gestured that Georgiana was present and Mama had tucked her book under her arm and said stiffly that they would discuss it later. Once Mama had gone, Papa winked at Georgiana who'd assumed her mother was worrying about nothing, otherwise Papa would have taken it seriously. Mama always found things to fuss about. If Papa spent a lot of money on travelling and on scientific equipment, then it must be for a good reason.

However, Papa didn't restrict his spending to travel and scientific instruments, he had expensive tastes and was often extravagant, buying gifts for his wife and daughter as well as objets d'art for their house. When he'd asked Gianfranco to paint the family, he'd asked for a magnificent group portrait and three separate miniatures which had jewel-encrusted frames.

Papa had sat first for his portrait. He'd chosen his study as a setting and when it was finished, everyone agreed the likeness was amazing. Mama sat next for Gianfranco in her sitting room on her favourite chair. Again, the likeness was astonishing. Mama sat upright with her small pug on her lap, her blonde hair in an elaborate style with soft ringlets falling to her shoulders and her round face relaxed and confident.

The trouble began when it was time for Georgiana to sit. She'd chosen the garden and all had gone well until Mama wanted to see how Gianfranco was progressing.

'Such a pretty child,' Gianfranco said in his strong Italian accent. He stood back for Mama to admire his work. 'And she bears such a resemblance to her father.'

Georgiana had been pleased. How wonderful to know she looked like her father, the man she adored. But Mama had alternated between staring at the painting and at her daughter; brows drawn as she scrutinised both. Gianfranco stood back to allow her to see his work, his expression proud, knowing he'd captured a perfect likeness. 'I disagree,' Mama said finally. Her face drained of colour and hands pressed to her mouth as if she were viewing something frightful.

Gianfranco's expression registered dismay, 'Is it not to your liking, Cecile? I can alter anything ...' he faltered, noticing the two angry red spots on her cheeks.

'No, indeed!' she said angrily, 'Please carry on exactly as you are. In fact, I insist on it!' She turned on her heel and strode to the house.

Failing to understand why her mother had reacted in such an unexpected manner, Georgiana burst into tears. What had happened? Had she done something wrong? It couldn't have been Gianfranco's fault, Mama loved his paintings.

That night, Georgiana was served supper in her room. Downstairs, her parents were arguing. The shrill exclamations of her mother, punctuated by sobs and the deeper murmur of her father which eventually rose to angry shouts. Surely a tiny portrait couldn't be that important?

Mama's bedroom was directly below Georgiana's and the sound of sobbing and wailing drifted upwards during the night, making it impossible for her to sleep. She longed to creep downstairs and wrap her arms around Mama and ask for forgiveness for whatever she'd done but she dared not. Mama's expression as she'd glanced at her daughter before she'd walked away from the easel had been one she had never seen on her mother's face before and fear gnawed at her, making her start at every noise. Eventually, exhaustion overtook her and she slept, waking late. Ella, the maid, hadn't woken her and as the previous day's baffling events crowded back into her mind, she got up, put on her wrap and rushed downstairs. Perhaps everything hadn't been as bad as it had sounded last night?

Her mother's bedroom door was closed but as she rushed downstairs, she heard Papa's voice in the entrance hall. He was talking to the staff and Georgiana heard Ella snivelling.

'Papa!' she said, running as fast as she could down the stairs, 'Where are you going?'

He stooped to hug her and holding her face in his hands, he kissed her forehead, 'I have to go away, my darling. Look after Mama for me.'

'But Papa, why can't you look after Mama?'

'I'll explain to you one day, Georgiana. But not today. I have to catch a coach. And it's best I go quickly before ...'

He broke off, unable to finish the sentence and Georgiana threw her arms around his neck. If she could hold tightly enough, he wouldn't go.

'Please, my lovely, I have to go. You're making this harder for us both,' he said in such a way she had to unclasp her hands and free him.

'Papa?' Her breath caught in her throat as he nodded to the servants to pick up his trunk. Putting on his hat, he turned and walked out.

Georgiana never saw nor heard from him again. Shortly after he'd left, Mama said he'd had a riding accident and died. Weeks went by and no one mentioned a funeral. It wasn't until many years later, she realised that Papa would have had some sort of burial and that it was simply that she and Mama hadn't gone.

After Papa left, Mama spent days in bed, barely eating and not responding when her daughter tried to comfort her. In fact, Georgiana's presence seemed to make her more agitated.

Without her mother running the household or keeping an eye on the accounts, Georgiana was aware of servants whispering among themselves and arguing on the kitchen doorstep with men who were demanding payment. One by one, they left, until only Cook, the butler and Ella remained. Mama had roused herself at that point and spent hours at her desk writing letters, one of which summoned her sister, Alice, and husband, Thomas, to their house. Ella was instructed to take Georgiana for a walk and by the time they arrived back at the house, Mama had gone to her room and Aunt Alice appeared to be in charge.

During the following few days, people came and went, valuable paintings and vases were removed and Georgiana's clothes were packed in a chest ready for the journey to Aunt Alice's home in the country. If it hadn't been for Ella informing her that the house in London was to be sold to pay off Papa's debts and that she and Mama would be living at Aunt Alice's house in the future, Georgiana wouldn't have known what was happening. It was as if she was invisible. Men took paintings off walls, furniture from each room and china and cutlery from the kitchen until the house was almost bare. Then she and Mama rode in silence in the coach that Aunt Alice sent.

Shortly after they'd moved in with Aunt Alice in her mansion in the middle of the Essex countryside, Mama had an apoplectic fit. She took to her bed and after that, she seemed to lose interest in everything. Georgiana was raised with her cousin, Margaret, and later, her baby cousin, John. But it was always understood that Georgiana was inferior to Aunt Alice's children and when John was old enough, Georgiana became his unpaid carer. Not that she minded because John was a sweet child whom everyone loved. His blonde curls and big blue eyes gave him the appearance of an angel, much like his sister, Margaret, who he greatly resembled. His sister, however, although angelic in appearance, was nothing like it in disposition.

Georgiana now held the miniature of her father to her lips again and with a sigh, she put it back in the chest. Lieutenant Brooks hadn't mentioned bringing him food but when he came back, he'd expect her to have taken the bedding up to the main deck to air and since a glance out of the tiny cabin window revealed heavy clouds on the horizon, she decided to do it immediately.

When she got back to the cabin, Lieutenant Brooks was engrossed in his books and barely glanced up as she entered. How could this be the same man who had held her in his arms as they watched the blue spectacle in the sea?

When she went to fetch the bedding, she leaned over the gunwale where she'd been the previous evening and stared down at the grey, foam-flecked sea. Nothing of the blue phenomenon remained. The man had changed. The sea had changed. There was nothing to reassure her she hadn't dreamed the entire experience.

Along the deck, a sailor watched her as he whittled a stick with a knife. 'Lost something?'

Georgiana turned. It was the man who'd pestered her a few nights before.

She hauled her bedding out of the nets and rushed back to the cabin, with his laugh ringing in her ears.

★ ★ ★

The heat and humidity increased as the Lady Amelia crossed the Atlantic towards Rio de Janeiro and calm conditions alternated with squally, tropical storms preventing the convicts from exercising on deck. In the cramped, humid conditions, two women contracted gaol fever and Surgeon Joseph Dawson ordered them to be moved into his cramped hospital aft of the prison. Lieutenant Brooks visited several times and told Georgiana how the patients were faring.

'Joseph doesn't hold out much hope for the elder, but the younger one might survive. He's recommended cleaning the prison quarters as soon as we can to stop the disease spreading. We're going to explode small heaps of gunpowder throughout the deck to disperse the noxious vapours and once that's done, it'll be whitewashed with quicklime and cleaned with oil of tar again. But we need better weather first. We can't get all the convicts up on the main deck in this storm.' He glanced at the small cabin window but it was impossible to see out because of the torrential rain lashing against the panes.

By mid-afternoon, the heavy rain clouds had blown away and the fierce sun beat down, drying the deck and the sails. Captain Yeats ordered the convicts to be brought up to the main deck to exercise while the gunpowder was exploded to clean the air and once everything had dried after being coated in quicklime and oil of tar, the women were allowed back down to their quarters, just as the leaden clouds blew towards them, obscuring the evening sun and threatening further storms.

Joseph Dawson joined the lieutenant in his cabin that evening and they ate their meal together, completing logs and going over the lists of stores. Someone had discovered several of the casks of fresh water which they'd loaded in Santa

Cruz had leaked and were now empty. With the alternating calms and storms impeding their progress, it was unlikely they'd make Rio before the drinking water ran out unless it was rationed.

'Captain Yeats will let the men know it'll be only three pints of fresh water for drinking per person per day,' the surgeon said, 'From tomorrow. All washing will have to be done in sea water.'

Georgiana was not included in the conversation but she listened in as they discussed rats, lice, fleas, and low water supplies.

'If we don't get to Rio soon, we'll have to start rationing food,' Joseph said.

'D'you think we've halted the gaol fever?' Lieutenant Brooks asked.

Surgeon Dawson shook his head, 'I'd be most surprised if there weren't many more.'

The doctor was correct. The two victims had been in proximity to many others before they showed symptoms and the following days saw the disease pass to four women and a sailor.

* ★ ★

One evening several days later, three seamen came to the lieutenant in his cabin to complain they'd been given short rations and to ask him to investigate. He assured them he'd make enquiries and sort the matter out on the morrow.

They were followed by the bosun who wanted to report an unusual amount of damage in the stores by the rats and to enquire how much vinegar had been on board when they'd sailed.

The lieutenant ran his finger across the entry in his book, 'We set sail from England with four hundred gallons. Is there a shortage?'

'There's definitely not as much in the stores as there should be,' the bosun said and Lieutenant Brooks promised to look into it after he'd enquired about the men's rations.

Georgiana poured the two men brandy and they talked for some time, discussing the rat problem and how much vinegar and other necessities they would need to buy in Rio. Supplies of fresh vegetables were low and the bosun said there'd been several cases of scurvy among the crew.

When the bosun had gone, Lieutenant Brooks leaned back in his chair, stretched out his legs and yawned. He'd been up before dawn and there were dark smudges under his eyes.

'Surgeon Dawson had two more cases of gaol fever this morning,' he said, 'It seems to be slowing down but I hope that's the last of them, the poor man's exhausted and I miss his good sense and assistance.'

'You seem very tired too,' Georgiana said, then ventured, 'Do... do you think I might offer to help the surgeon? I'm used to nursing my mother,' she added quickly, in an attempt to add creditability to her offer, 'Marna had apoplexy years ago and for a while she lost the use of one side of her body. She's improved although she's still not strong. I looked after her until ...' she paused, 'until I was imprisoned.'

He put his pen down and turned to

look at her, 'I'm very sorry to hear that. I didn't realise,' he said gently, 'Who's looking after her now?'

Georgiana lowered her head, 'My cousin and aunt, I hope. At least, they promised they would.'

'Is there reason to doubt your aunt and cousin will keep their promise?'

'I don't know. I hope not.'

Aunt Alice she trusted, but Margaret? Georgiana knew her cousin did exactly as she pleased and if the promise she'd made didn't suit her, she was quite capable of ignoring it.

★ ★ ★

After Georgiana had brought the lieutenant his morning meal, she washed the clothes in sea water, aired the blankets and tidied the cabin then made her way to the hospital where he'd arranged for her to help Surgeon Dawson. She was, grateful she didn't have to walk through the prison quarters to get to the hospital because several of the women displayed jealousy of her elevated position as the Naval Agent's sea-wife by barging her out of the way in the queue for food and loudly making ribald comments about her whenever they saw her.

Surgeon Dawson glanced up from the patient he was examining when Georgiana entered the hospital. Like the prison quarters, it was dark and cramped with foetid air and barely room to stand up. This was going to be very different from nursing Mama in her sunny bedroom in Aunt Alice's house.

'Dinah, I need more clean blankets. Georgiana's come to help us, so take her with you and bring back fresh water, please. And some more vinegar,' he said to the woman who was wiping a patient's forehead with a damp cloth. Georgiana recognised her as the first woman who'd caught the fever and had recovered. Three others lay moaning or crying out for water, their faces covered in sweat. A sixth patient lay motionless, her eyes open as if staring at the ceiling.

Dinah's lip curled in scorn. Presumably she shared the others' contempt for the sea-wife.

'Here,' she said, handing Georgiana a pile of bedding and taking the others herself. She silently led the way to the top deck and the two women tied the blankets to ropes and lowered them overboard to be dragged along and washed by the sea. While Georgiana kept an eye on them, Dinah sat on the deck, her shoulders slumped and head bowed. She was obviously still weak from her illness. Without waking her, Georgiana hauled the blankets back onboard and after wringing them out, she suspended them in the netting to dry. Dinah woke, bleary eyed when a sailor rolled a barrel past her whistling noisily and she unsteadily got to her feet.

'Why didn't you wake me?' she asked crossly.

'There was no need,' Georgiana said with a smile. 'I managed.'

Dinah was obviously not going to be. won over easily. She merely regarded Georgiana suspiciously, checked the blankets were fast in the rigging, then shrugged and jerked her head to indicate that Georgiana should accompany her

Dinah fetched the vinegar then filled the pitchers with fresh water from the enormous barrel and handed one to Georgiana to carry, all the time avoiding eye contact. Without comment, she led the way back to the hospital.

'Shall I hold her while you put the cup to her lips?' Georgiana asked when Dinah tried to raise the patient's head with one hand and hold the cup to her mouth with the other.

Dinah shrugged but allowed Georgiana to do as she'd suggested and they moved to the next patient. The woman who'd been lying motionless earlier had disappeared and the only evidence Georgiana could see of her having been there, was a pile of dirty bedding which Dinah cleared away with a slow shake of her head.

Dinah saw the direction of her gaze, 'I didn't think she'd make it,' she commented, 'That's another one they'll blame me for.' She nodded in the direction of the convict women's quarters.

'But it wasn't your fault!'

'It was me what give 'em the fever..'

'Surgeon Dawson says it's not passed from one person to another. He said he thinks it's something to do with fleas or ticks. So you couldn't have passed it on.'

Dinah smiled, 'Kind of you to say,' she said sadly, 'but the others don't see it like that.' She shrugged and moved to the next patient, lifting her head gently so Georgiana could hold the cup to her lips.

'It's faster doing it like this,' she said, 'and not so easy to spill the water.' The earlier offhand tone had gone and for the first time, it seemed as though her frostiness might have thawed.

★　★　★

The middle watch began at midnight and when the bell sounded, Georgiana suggested Surgeon Dawson go back to his cabin for a few hours' sleep. He was obviously exhausted. Dinah was already asleep, curled up in the corner. When he returned at four o'clock to take over, Georgiana went to her bed, promising to return at the beginning of the next watch at eight. Throughout the following days, they took it in shifts to care for the patients and on the day before the Lady Amelia was due to reach Brazil, Surgeon Dawson reported to Georgiana when she arrived at the hospital in the morning that there had been no new cases of fever for the third day in a row.

Six patients had died and now only two remained in the hospital. Surgeon Dawson was certain one would survive although the fate of the other hung in the balance. She alternated between sweating and shivering uncontrollably. Gaunt before she'd caught the fever, it seemed unlikely she'd withstand the ravages of the disease, yet she clung on with a steely tenacity.

Dinah's initial hostility towards Georgiana had waned as the days passed until she'd acquired a grudging acceptance for her helpfulness amid the stench of sickness and death. The two women worked well together and Surgeon Dawson had begun to rely on them.

He informed them that if the southeast trade winds continued to speed them on their journey, Captain Yeats expected the ship to reach Rio de Janeiro by late afternoon the following day. Since the convict women had been well behaved recently with no fighting or disturbances, the master had decided they'd be allowed on shore for a few hours with the men who were not on watch. Whether the good behaviour had been the result of lack of stamina due to sickness and reduced rations, it was hard to say, nevertheless, it was being rewarded with a trip ashore.

As Surgeon Dawson would have ample opportunity to visit the city while they were at anchor, he proposed he stay onboard and look after the patients — by that time, there might only be one patient or perhaps none — and his two nursing assistants would be able to go ashore with the party when the ship anchored.

'Let's hope the trade winds carry us to shore speedily,' the doctor said, 'We urgently need fresh food and drinking water.'

★ ★ ★

The winds continued to drive the Lady Amelia towards the city of San Sebastian de Rio de Janeiro and the following day just after noon, the lookout yelled from his vantage point high in the rigging, to report he could see the shores of Brazil. Georgiana and Dinah joined the crowd on the main deck for their first glimpse of land in many weeks, watching as the mist lifted to reveal mountains and forests, then greater detail, such as the fort at the harbour mouth.

'We'll dine ashore, tonight, sweetheart,' Lieutenant Brooks said as he came up behind Georgiana and put his arm around her. It was for show, of course. He'd taken to calling her 'sweetheart' when others were around and she called him Francis. Yet still, she leaned into him enjoying the feel of her back against his chest.

Dinah was fond of saying, 'Take yer pleasures where yer can. Yer don't know how long you've got on this earth.' And Georgiana knew the girl had heeded her own advice and formed an affection for one of the midshipmen, Philip Martin. Dinah knew nothing could come of the relationship because, like Lieutenant Brooks, Philip would be sailing with the Lady Amelia for China. Nevertheless, she slipped away with the midshipman at every opportunity.

Georgiana leaned her head against Francis' chest and allowed herself a few seconds of pretence. Too soon, he pulled away and with a kiss on her forehead, he told her to be on deck ready to leave with the first longboat to shore, and he would meet her there.

She smiled as she brushed her hair and pinned it up under her cap: At least she had her own clothes and didn't feel too dowdy. Some of the convicts had also brought boxes, chests and bags but she had no idea if they'd be allowed access to them so they could change out of their striped prison garb. Taking the black fan the lieutenant had bought her in Tenerife, she was ready. There was no full-length looking glass, merely a small mirror Lieutenant Brooks used when he shaved and it was too small to see herself. She would have to do. After all, it didn't really matter. No one would even notice.

* * *

The longboats were lowered over the side of the Lady Amelia when she dropped anchor in the harbour and members of the crew who weren't on watch and convict women gathered in an excited crowd waiting to be transferred to shore.

Lieutenant Brooks, as the Naval Agent, accompanied the ship's master in the first longboat to leave, along with Georgiana, senior officers and paying passengers. She was disappointed to learn that although she'd spend the evening with Francis, she'd be sent back to the ship with the other convict women while the master, officers and passengers would attend a reception at the Viceroy's Palace. It would have been foolish to have imagined otherwise and she knew she was lucky to be included in Captain Yeats' party in the first longboat. Reverend Leston, his wife and the other passengers chatted together but turned their backs on Georgiana to make it clear they wanted nothing to do with her. She surreptitiously looked to see if Francis was disturbed by their behaviour but he was deep in conversation with Captain Yeats and if he'd noticed, gave no sign.

Georgiana concentrated on the sights and sounds of San Sebastian which the longboat was rapidly approaching. Judging by the cacophony of pealing bells and the many towers that soared above the roofs, the city had a vast array of churches and religious buildings.

Lieutenant Brooks smiled when he saw

her puzzled expression as she stumbled while stepping onto the shore, 'Don't worry, you'll feel unsteady for a while but it isn't permanent. It usually takes a few days to disappear. Once you're in Sydney …' he stopped abruptly, 'Well, anyway, there's no need to worry.'

Their destination had been the last thing she wanted to think about on an evening when she'd temporarily been set free to roam through an exciting city on the arm of a kind and thoughtful man. She could tell from his expression he'd regretted mentioning Sydney, reminding her of the future he knew she was dreading. He offered her his arm, patting her hand when she took it as if to comfort. her and she smiled up at him. There was nothing she could do to control the future or the past. Her only option was to live in the present and take heed of Dinah's philosophy, seizing her pleasure where she could.

She soon forgot the strange rocking sensation in her legs as they explored the streets. The city was laid out geometrically, with roads running parallel to each other and intersecting at right angles. It was nothing like London with its rabbit warren of tiny alleys that criss-crossed each other in a seemingly random manner. Images of the Virgin Mary were displayed on many of the street corners and people frequently stopped to pray and sing, their voices vying with the church bells and babble of Portuguese which was everywhere.

She wondered if Papa had been as excited as she was now when he'd visited Europe. If so, then she could understand why he'd spent so much time travelling. Despite his stories, she'd had no idea how different everything was from the life they had in London. The people seemed larger than life with mannerisms, fashions and a language which were all unfamiliar. Even the smells were different with aromatic spices and fragrances she couldn't identify filling the air. She couldn't believe the number of shops lining the streets and the range of goods they sold, nor the profusion of churches, convents and monasteries with their monks, nuns and ministers.

Lieutenant Brooks and Georgiana reached a large plaza at the same time as the doors of a church opened and from the dark interior, the congregation poured out into the evening sunshine. At the head of the worshippers were eight bearers carrying a statue of the patron saint on their shoulders which swayed from side to side as they descended the church steps and crossed the square, their pace in time to the slow, steady beat of a drum. Men in white robes, with rosaries in their hands, walked behind the statue, chanting as they went, their heads bowed and their feet bare.

The couple followed the procession as it made its way along a wide avenue, with onlookers crowded on each side crossing themselves and muttering prayers. Above, on balconies and at ornate windows people gathered and threw petals onto the crowd below, filling the air with colour and scent.

'This is glorious!' Georgiana said,

'For the second time in my life, I've seen a marvel and both times it's been with you!'

As they strolled along the avenues and streets, they reached an easy familiarity she knew would disappear as soon as they were back aboard the ship but now their blossoming friendship added to the atmosphere and intoxication of the evening.

When the procession had passed, Francis led her back to the plaza, to a whitewashed inn with brilliant flowers at the windows.

'Tonight, let's have something other than salt pork and bread as hard as wood!' he said to Georgiana, as the innkeeper led them to a table in the courtyard.

★ ★ ★

The evening was warm and as darkness descended, the innkeeper's wife brought lanterns into the courtyard, placing one on each table. The meal and wine had been delicious and Georgiana felt full for the first time since she'd been at Aunt Alice's house. Francis had been attentive and amusing company but she knew when he took out his pocket watch he would soon take her to the harbour where he'd leave her and then carry on to the palace.

'Oh dear,' she said with a mock serious expression as he checked his watch, 'I must be losing my touch.' When he looked at her quizzically, she smiled and nodded at the watch, 'You have such a valuable item, and I still haven't managed to relieve you of it.'

He laughed. 'I apologised at the time for jumping to conclusions about you stealing my ring. I can do no more than that.'

She was relieved he'd taken her words in jest as she'd intended but not so happy to see what appeared to be a shadow pass across his eyes.

'Well, as pleasant as this has been,' he said rising and calling the innkeeper; 'We must leave now if you're to be in time for the longboat and I am to make the reception.'

'Francis,' she said as they walked back towards the harbour, 'thank you for this evening. I know you're only fulfilling your duty but you've done it with such generosity and kindness. This evening has been a highlight I shall remember. Indeed, I can't think of a time when I've been happier, except perhaps when my father was alive. But that was so long ago.'

Her hand was on his arm and without saying anything, he placed his hand over hers and squeezed.

★ ★ ★

Francis waited until the longboat containing Georgiana glided out into the harbour before he turned towards the Viceroy's Palace. He was slightly late but if he hurried, he was sure he'd make it in time. Around him, the city bustled, alive with garrulous people strolling and enjoying the balmy night. But now Georgiana had gone, the streets seemed less colourful, less vibrant.

That evening, he'd spent several hours with her and he was convinced he'd seen the real Georgiana — a quick witted, intelligent, warm hearted woman. Nevertheless, Thomas' words of warning that she was deceitful and untrustworthy gnawed at him. She'd offered to work in the hospital with Joseph who was full of praise for her diligence and kindness. Could a woman be so cunning as to fool them both? Surely, he'd misunderstood Thomas.

Francis reminded himself that it didn't really matter if she was dishonest or not because he'd never see her again once they'd docked in Sydney Cove. The crushing weight of disappointment bore down upon him.

He arrived at the palace in time to join the party from the Lady Amelia led by Captain Yeats who'd taken his passengers on a tour around the city. Francis was pleased to see most of them had arrived at the palace after him, and that he wasn't the last to join the queue to enter the reception room to be introduced to the Viceroy.

'Ah, Lieutenant Brooks! I trust you've had a passable time ashore this evening? In truth, my daughter and I were rather shocked at the shameless displays of popery.' Mr Chesterton, the Quaker, who was on his way to Canton in China with his daughter, sucked in his cheeks in indignation, making his already gaunt face appear even more skeletal.

'I had a very agreeable time, thank you, Mr Chesterton,' Francis said politely. He didn't want to spend more time than was necessary with the puritanical man, nor with his daughter. Miss Chesterton had sat next to Francis at the last dinner Captain Yeats had hosted and had spent most of the evening talking about her father's plans to travel throughout China with the purpose of spreading his religious views. Francis found everything about her sharp. Her face was hollow cheeked like her father's, with thin lips which she often clamped together when she disapproved of something — which appeared to be much of the time.

'I found the city quite deplorable!' she said, inserting· her angular frame between the two men, 'My father has travelled extensively and he's described similar disgraceful displays but I must admit, Lieutenant Brooks, they still took me quite by surprise. Obviously, you didn't see the procession we witnessed or you'd feel the same. One could hardly move for people praying to idols of the Virgin Mary on every street corner.'

'Yes, I saw a procession,' Francis said, glancing over her shoulder to see how much longer he'd have to wait to be presented to the Viceroy and listen to Miss Chesterton's opinions. 'I thought it was most colourful.'

'But, surely, Lieutenant,' Mr Chesterton said tapping his chin with a bony finger in the manner which Francis recognised from earlier conversations to mean that he was anticipating an argument, 'you can't believe a religious event should be handled in such an ostentatious way. Acts of worship should be dignified and quiet.'

'I bow to your superior knowledge,' Francis said, inclining his head and stepping away from the determined man. They were next in line to meet the Viceroy and once the introductions were concluded, he would excuse himself and avoid the couple. But Miss Chesterton had not finished.

'And what did your ...' she faltered, 'Your convict servant think of the idolatry and pageantry?'

Francis suppressed a smile at her euphemistic use of the term convict servant. Without mentioning the words sea-wife, she'd acknowledged Georgiana as such because no one would enquire about the opinions of a servant.

'She had similar views to me,' Francis said, knowing he hadn't actually expressed an opinion. The last thing he wanted was a religious argument.

Miss Chesterton sniffed. It appeared she wasn't really enquiring about Georgiana's thoughts but rather wanted to somehow introduce her into the conversation. 'I see. While we are on the subject, if you don't mind me saying, your em ... living arrangements are rather a cause for comment among the passengers.'

'Really?' Fraricis raised his eyebrows.

'Do you have a wife in England, Lieutenant?'

'No, Miss Chesterton, I do not.'

He noticed the glimmer of a smile on her narrow lips.

'And am I right in thinking your em ... servant will be leaving you in Sydney?'

'That is correct.'

'I see. Reputations can easily be damaged, you know. A remedy to that could be marriage to a suitable woman. Someone of good character.'

'May I present Mr and Miss Chesterton, passengers bound for China, your excellency,' Captain Yeats said, giving Francis an excuse to avoid replying. His initial irritation at her rudeness was suddenly quashed by the suspicion that when she said someone of good character, she was referring to herself and he determined to keep his distance from the overbearing woman.

Once Miss Chesterton had been introduced, she waited for Francis but the
Viceroy was so deeply in conversation
with the Naval Agent, that eventually,
Mr Chesterton led his daughter away to
join the other guests.

Francis managed to keep out of the
Chestertons way for the rest of the
evening and ensured the father and
daughter boarded the longboat first
while he was in the last. By the time
Francis got on deck, the passengers had
gone to their cabins.

★ ★ ★

The longboat back to the Lady Amelia
had been crowded with convict women
crushed together. Georgiana huddled
on the hard, wooden seat, with her head
lowered to avoid drawing attention to
herself. However, most of the women
had eaten and drunk their fill for the
first time in many weeks and were too
happy to bother baiting the sea-wife they
envied and resented.

Several women sang raucously and risked capsizing the boat with their attempts to dance before one of the sailors knocked them back into their seats with his oar.

Georgiana breathed a sigh of relief when the longboat reached the ship without anyone noticing her. Bosun George Clark, waited on deck, checking each woman off his list as they boarded and when Georgiana heard him call Dinah's name, she looked up, hoping to catch sight of her. It would be nice to see a friendly face, but once Dinah was aboard, she disappeared from view among the growing crowd of women who, with much shrieking and laughter were jostling each other and staggering about. The bosun's voice became louder and sharper, trying to maintain order as more women climbed up onto the deck, joining the drunken melee. Dinah reappeared further along the deck, looking back over her shoulder at the group and seconds later, Georgiana realised why. From the shadows, Midshipman Philip

Martin appeared and the pair slipped away. There would be no opportunity to speak to Dinah that night.

With her eyes still drawn to the spot where Dinah and Philip had embraced, Georgiana saw the sailor who had hit her the evening before they set sail from Tenerife. She'd seen him several times since that although he hadn't harassed her again. On one occasion while she was helping in the hospital, the sailor had come in to see Surgeon Dawson who'd looked inside his mouth, glanced at the bruises on his arms, smelled his breath and diagnosed scurvy. He'd prescribed essence of malt and given the man mercury drops and ointment which Georgiana knew was prescribed for venereal conditions. She'd shivered with disgust at the thought of the sailor having pushed himself so close to her.

'Another sailor who can't keep himself to himself,' Surgeon Dawson had said shaking his head disapprovingly once the man had gone.

'Who is he?' she'd asked.

'Arthur Towler. He's the carpenter's mate. If you want my advice, keep well out of his way. He's not popular among the men and there have already been accusations made against him by several of the women. Bearing in mind many of the complaints have been made by the hardest and most ruthless women I've ever met, I can't imagine what he did to them. Towler is a thoroughly disagreeable man and a rogue. In fact, I imagine many of the convicts aboard the ship are more honest than him.'

Now as Georgiana prepared to climb out of the longboat, Arthur Towler was looking over the gunwale directly at her, his mouth twisted in what passed as a smile. Then slowly, he licked his flabby lips.

Georgiana shuddered, involuntarily stepping backwards onto the foot of a sailor who swore loudly and shoved her, sending her sprawling. He shouted at her to get up and grabbing her by the jacket, hoisted her to her feet. When she looked up at the deck again, Towler had gone and she hurried to the deck, hoping to lose herself in the disorderly crowd. But as Bosun Clark ticked her off on his list, another officer and sailors rounded up the women and escorted them to their deck, leaving her alone.

'Get along to your cabin, now, Miss,' the bosun said. He would be aware that as she was under the protection of Lieutenant Brooks, he couldn't speak to her with the same indifference as the other convicts, yet he obviously couldn't bring himself to treat her like a paying passenger.

She was about to appeal to him to accompany her to the cabin when there was a scream and the sound of shouts coming from the direction of the convicts. He swore loudly and strode briskly away, leaving her alone.

Below there were men still on the longboat and she could see a group of sailors further along the deck smoking pipes and relaxing but no sign of Arthur Towler. With thudding heart, she headed to the cabin, eyes wide with the effort of seeing in the dark. As one of the ship's cats darted out from behind a cask and chased a rat across the deck; she stifled a scream and flattened herself against a large crate, her heart beating so hard her ears were filled with the sound of each thump.

Stop being foolish! Get to the cabin quickly. He won't dare interfere with you ...

When her heart had slowed a little, she hurried to the cabin but to her horror, Towler had beaten her to it and was lounging against the door, blocking her way. She stopped abruptly, with her breath coming in short, sharp gasps.

Don't let him see you're afraid.

Instinctively, she knew fear would encourage him. Willing her face to appear calm and her voice steady, she said in as imperious a manner as she could, 'Please move. You're blocking my way.'

Surprisingly, he took his arm away from the door and stepped to one side.

''Ow about a little kiss?' he whined ...

She ignored his words and strode purposefully to the cabin but when she drew

113

level with him, he grabbed her wrist and jerked her towards him. 'Ships can be dangerous places. Accidents 'appen all the time. If your lieutenant should be in the wrong place at the wrong time ... I 'ate to think what might 'appen. And who'd look out fer you then? Of course, if you were a bit accommodating, I could keep an eye on 'im and make sure no 'arm came to 'im.' He leaned towards her and she shrank back at the stench of his breath. Without thinking, she brought her knee up sharply, making contact with his groin. He flung her wrist away and bent double groaning and cursing.

With trembling fingers, she fumbled at the latch. With a jolt, it opened and she threw herself inside, slamming the door behind her and pushing Francis' chair against it. Towler didn't attempt to follow her and with her ear to the door, she heard his curses recede until it appeared he'd gone. Fear knotted her stomach: Arthur Towler didn't seem the kind of man who'd forget such an insult. Georgiana looked around the cabin for a weapon but there was nothing small enough to be practical for her to take to bed, nor large enough to offer a threat should Towler return. She could wait up until Francis came back but if he found her awake, he might demand to know why she hadn't gone to bed and she feared she wouldn't be able to convince him that all was well. She'd already behaved foolishly in hurting Towler although it was possible he'd now leave her alone. She'd seen it in prison; the strong targeting the weak until one of them fought back and earned the bully's respect.

A search of the cabin revealed very little to use as a weapon except her hair brush. It would be better than nothing although it wasn't very heavy. She wondered if Francis' silver hair brush would be more substantial. It would mean taking it out of his chest but he slept soundly and she knew she'd be able to return it before he woke and discovered she'd borrowed it.

As she was reaching in to his chest to get the hair brush, she caught sight of his shaving box. A razor would be a good weapon. She knew at least one of the women in prison had carried one for protection before she'd been arrested. Not that Georgiana planned to use it but if Towler returned, he would surely take the threat of a blade more seriously than a hairbrush. She opened the box and slipped her finger beneath the bone-handled razor and prising it from the satin lining, she laid it on the palm of her hand. It gleamed in the lantern light and she felt sick at the thought of threatening anyone with it, let alone using it.

Undressing to her shift, she climbed into bed, with the bone handle of the razor nestling in her hand. It occurred to her that she ought to have opened it before she'd blown out the candle so she was familiar with it. Easing the blade out of the handle, she opened the razor. It had been easier than expected and she was confident she'd be ready if necessary. When she tried to push the blade back into the handle, it snapped shut faster than she'd expected and sliced into her middle finger. It had barely touched her, yet she could taste blood when she sucked at the wound. While she waited for it to stop bleeding, she wondered how long Francis would be. As soon as he returned, she'd have to wait until he was asleep before returning the razor to its box and she began to wonder if it had been wise to take it in the first place. Another thought occurred to her — suppose he didn't return to the ship that night? He hadn't said he would. She'd simply assumed he'd come back.

Several men walked past the door, their voices low and resonant and Georgiana tensed, ready to free the blade on the razor if they tried the door but the sound of bare feet on wood and the rumble as one of them laughed grew fainter.

Just as she was considering the possibility she might have to remain awake all night, she heard Francis' voice. He bade the Quaker's daughter good night and lifted the latch. She barely had time to lay down and feign sleep, the razor hidden in the folds of her shift.

It didn't take Francis long to undress and climb into bed and then shortly after, she heard his rhythmic breathing. Georgiana lay there for some time wanting to be certain he was deeply asleep before she attempted to return his razor. Every creak of the ship, every squeak, rasp or scrape of rats or cats outside the door jarred her nerves until it felt as though her skull was being crushed. She slowly swung her legs to the ground and remained immobile for a count of thirty, then transferring her weight to them, she stood up and crept gingerly across the floor to the chest. As she drew level with his face, he snorted and turned over, settling down again with a loud sigh. She waited until his breathing became regular, then tiptoed on. The hinges of the chest squealed as she raised the lid and she froze, holding her breath, her heart thudding, but still, he didn't stir. Sweat trickled down her back but there was no stopping now, She dared not raise the lid higher, so she inserted one hand and after groping inside, she found the shaving box. With her shoulder bracing the lid of the chest, she pulled the box out, raised the lid, slipped the razor back into the satin interior and quietly closed it.

You're nearly there!

She bit her bottom lip as she lowered the chest lid, praying it wouldn't squeal and although the hinges grated, the noise wasn't sufficient to arouse him. By the time she reached her bed, she was almost sobbing with relief.

★　★　★

As a parting gift to the ship's master, the viceroy sent several boxes of oranges and once back onboard, Captain Yeats invited those who'd accompanied him to the palace, to help themselves. The rest, he said, would be divided up between the crew on the morrow.

Francis took three oranges. One for himself and two for Georgiana. He hoped it would make up for missing the reception. Not that she'd missed much but he was sure in other circumstances, she'd have enjoyed the occasion.

He intended to seek out Bosun Clark who'd been charged with ensuring all the convicts were safely back in their quarters before he went to bed and he wanted to ask about Georgiana. He knew all the women who'd been claimed as sea-wives by officers were victimised by the other convicts who resented their temporary elevation in status. Francis wished he'd thought to make sure Georgiana had been in the longboat with the other sea-wives but until that evening, he hadn't realised so many officers had taken their pick of the women. Presumably, as the voyage progressed, more officers would take a fancy to a particular woman and since Captain Yeats appeared to grudgingly accept the practice, there was no obstacle. He started to skirt the group of passengers, some of whom were already paring off orange peel with penknives and devouring the fruit, when he realised he'd have to pass Miss Chesterton and her father to leave the captain's cabin. They were talking to Reverend Leston although Francis could see Miss Chesterton's eyes were roaming across the faces of those assembled as though searching for someone. He drew back behind tall Mr Everton, the school teacher and waited for an opportunity to pass the Quaker couple without being seen. Once the oranges had been consumed, many bid their fellow passengers good night and returned to their quarters. If Francis didn't go soon, he'd be left with the Lestons and the Chestertons who were discussing the religious procession they'd witnessed earlier. Francis slipped out from behind Mr Everton and was about to go back to his cabin when Miss Chesterton spotted him and excusing herself from the conversation, she hurried towards him.

'Ah, Lieutenant Brooks, I wondered where you'd gone. What a thought provoking evening and a very pleasurable end to the night at the viceroy's residence. I understand we've all been invited to dine with his excellency on the eve of our departure! I shall look forward to learning all about the role of a Naval Agent, I overheard a little of your conversation with the viceroy.'

'Unfortunately, I won't be able to attend the dinner,' Francis said, 'I'm afraid I shall be too busy that evening preparing for the voyage.'

Miss Chesterton arranged her thin lips into a pout, 'Oh, that is a shame. But how is it, if things are so busy, that Captain Yeats can be spared?'

'Captain Yeats has arranged to attend for an hour or so and then he too will return to the ship.' She glanced over his shoulder at her father and then presumably seeing him fully occupied, she placed a hand on Francis' arm, 'Surely you could be spared for an hour or two, like the captain?'

'Im afraid you overestimate my importance aboard ship, Miss Chesterton. Captain Yeats has many officers to do his bidding. I do not. In fact, I have to be at my duties now, so I fear I must bid you good night' He disengaged his arm.

'Well, Lieutenant, I wonder if you would do me the courtesy of accompanying me back to my cabin. I fear my father will be sharing his views for a while yet and I'm rather tired.'

Francis had no choice. His cabin was next to hers. 'Of course,' he said politely, and offered her his arm.

'I bid you good night,' he said as they arrived at her door and hastily turned before she could engage him in conversation again, and slipped into his room.

Georgiana was asleep. He undressed in the dark and got into bed.

When he woke, Georgiana was still asleep although very restless. Her breathing was shallow and rapid and she was frowning and flinching as if afraid. She was obviously having a bad dream and he wondered whether he should rouse her. Her eyes flew open and she gasped, jerking herself away from him as if he'd threatened her.

'Georgiana?' he whispered.

At the sound of his voice, the terrified expression faded and she stared at him as if she were trying to understand what was happening. 'It's all right,' he said, 'It was just a dream.' She exhaled and the tension went from her.

'I have two oranges for you,' he said and inexplicably, she burst into tears. He pulled her to him and held her face against his chest until she'd finished crying. 'If you don't like oranges, you don't have to eat them,' he said, hoping she'd laugh.

'That's really kind, thank you.'

At least she'd managed a smile. 'A bad dream?' he asked. She nodded.. 'It was too hot to sleep well last night,' he said, stroking her hair, 'I must admit, I don't feel well this morning. It'll be good to put to sea and feel the breeze on my face.'

'Thank you,' she said, pulling away and wiping the tears from her cheeks, 'I'd better get up and start work.'

'Don't hurry. I have to see the bosun. I won't be back until later.'

★ ★ ★

Francis returned to the cabin an hour later. Georgiana had left him a bowl of gruel on the desk and had presumably taken the bedding on deck to air.

Before he ate, he decided he'd shave. The early morning routine they'd got into earlier had been disrupted by his late night and her bad dream.

Taking his box out of the chest and opening it, he reached inside for the razor. For a moment, he wondered if the blade was stuck inside the handle when he realised his initials which were etched into the bone weren't visible. He turned the razor over. How strange that he'd put it back in the box upside down but then he'd been in a rush to go ashore the previous evening and perhaps hadn't paid much attention.

He probably would have forgotten it then, except that when he pulled the blade out, it had a dark smear on it which he realised was blood. He definitely hadn't cut himself the previous evening. Had someone borrowed his razor?

He'd ask Georgiana when she came

back if she knew if anyone had been in his cabin.

She returned shortly after, having hung the bedding and the washing out in the nets to dry and replied, quite nervously in his opinion, that if anyone had come in, she hadn't been aware of it. Francis offered her the oranges and she peeled one, wincing as the juice touched her hand. He noticed she had a long, thin, gash on her middle finger. The sort of cut which a finely honed blade might make. Surely, she hadn't been interfering with his possessions?

After shaving, he wiped his face with a cloth and rubbed his chin ruefully, 'I really must sharpen that razor,' he said as if to himself. Her cheeks reddened and she tucked her middle finger into her palm as if to conceal the cut, although she said nothing. Now he was sure she'd been holding his razor and had cut herself but why had she been using it?

A deep disquiet gnawed at him. He'd become convinced she was a good person who'd made wrong choices. She'd confessed and was being punished but deep down, she was decent. He'd concluded Thomas had been mistaken or perhaps he'd misunderstood Thomas. But now, he'd uncovered something extremely unsettling — that she'd been in possession of a weapon. Why?

★ ★ ★

Georgiana continued to eat the orange but its sweetness turned sour in her mouth and her finger stung. She dared not wipe it or draw his attention, to it. She was also aware she was blushing.

But the only way he could have known she'd taken his razor would have been if he'd woken while she was replacing it. And if he had, he'd surely have challenged her?

No, he couldn't possibly know, although if her cheeks didn't cool off, he might start asking questions. She turned away to hide her embarrassment and by the time she thought the redness had faded, he was ready to leave.

'I won't be back until late,' he said, in what she'd come to recognise as the voice he used when someone had angered him.

She wondered how late he'd be. Was he perhaps going ashore? The prospect of another night like the last loomed. Georgiana decided she'd tell Francis about Arthur Towler. After all, it was unlikely she could anger the odious sailor more than she had already, and if Francis knew he'd threatened to hurt him, perhaps Captain Yeats could make sure he didn't leave the ship at Sydney. Threatening an officer was a serious offence. As soon as Francis returned, she would tell him everything.

★ ★ ★

Francis was so deep in thought on his way to see Bosun Clark, he failed to take care as he climbed through the hatch and hit his head. He told himself he needed to focus on his job but he felt unusually tired and distracted.

I must be getting old.

Not long ago, he could have spent the night drinking and carousing with no ill effects the following day, but although he'd slept well, his head felt heavy. Perhaps it was the worry about Georgiana which was distracting him, making it hard to concentrate on work. If Georgiana meant someone harm, he needed to be one step ahead.

Only a fool would plan to maim or kill while aboard a ship. Georgiana had witnessed enough floggings to know there was no escape while at sea and everyone knew the punishment meted out by a ship's master was swift and brutal. Even while anchored, it would take a determined person to escape and survive successfully in a different country with no money or idea of local language or customs. No, she couldn't be planning anything violent. It simply didn't make sense. Nevertheless, he knew that if he was going to sleep easy again, he would have to keep his belongings, especially the razor, locked away.

Georgiana would notice his chest was locked, and if she was innocent, she would be hurt. If, however, she meant him or anyone else harm, he would need to be vigilant. She might no longer be able to get to his blade but there were many ways to hurt someone and for the first time, it occurred to him she could easily tamper with his food and drink, as she had access to the hospital medicine cabinet, including the poisons.

It was Georgiana who'd suggested offering to work in the hospital. Perhaps her motives hadn't been as selfless as he'd first believed.

If only he could think clearly! He had so many questions. How much poison was needed to kill someone? Georgiana could have concealed it in a pocket. How would one know if one had swallowed poison? Would there be symptoms or would one slide into unconsciousness and then death? After death, would anyone know it hadn't come about through natural causes?

Before he went to see the bosun,

he'd go to the hospital and ask Joseph. It would mean confiding in him about his suspicions but that would be a good thing because then there'd be two people keeping an eye on Georgiana. And Joseph could ensure he locked his medicines out of her reach.

Francis loosened his stock and opened the top of his shirt. It was insufferably hot today and already, beads of sweat stood out on his brow. It was early yet, so what temperature would be reached by noon? Sweat trickled into his eyes and he wiped them with his handkerchief but still, his vision was blurry and wouldn't clear. He drew his brows together, trying to focus but it was as if he were peering through water.

Then without warning, the world went black.

★ ★ ★

There was a knock at the cabin door. 'Surgeon sent me to bring you, Miss,' the ship's boy said to Georgiana, wiping his nose. on his sleeve, 'Right away, he said, Miss.'

Dinah had told her earlier that after the first night on shore, several sailors had reported to the surgeon with repeated bouts of vomiting. Presumably, he'd sent the ship's boy because he needed help with his patients.

The sour smell of sickness hung in the air as she entered the hospital and she shuddered as she anticipated what her day's work would entail. With its low beams and poor ventilation, the hospital would be unlikely to lose the stench for some time and she consoled herself with the thought that after a while, her nose would become accustomed to it.

Surgeon Dawson had his back to her and was bending over a patient. Two things struck Georgiana simultaneously — firstly the patient's trunk was covered in the rash which was typical of gaol fever and secondly ... the patient was Francis.

3

While Georgiana helped Francis put his shirt back on, a sailor entered complaining of vomiting and diarrhoea.

'Were you at Senhora Rosário's establishment last night?' Surgeon Dawson asked the wretched man, passing him a bucket.

The sailor nodded.

The surgeon shook his head and tutted, 'Well, I hope your evening with her ladies was worth it. And let's also hope this nasty sickness is the only one you brought away with you. I hear the girls she employs are none too clean.'

But the sailor wasn't listening. He was heaving, his head deep in the bucket.

'Shall I take Francis back to his cabin and care for him there?' Georgiana asked, 'You're going to be busy here.'

With his arm around Georgiana's shoulders, Francis was able to walk back to the cabin where she helped him undress and led him to her bed. He protested but she insisted she'd be fine on the floor and that he needed rest in a proper bed. She pulled a chair up to his bedside and wiped his face with a damp cloth.

Over the next few days, Dinah came with food and sat with Francis while Georgiana rested. Francis alternated between raging fever, and shivering chills and after each bout, he grew weaker and weaker.

Surgeon Dawson visited regularly and bled Francis but he told Georgiana he could do nothing other than keep him comfortable. Francis would either have the strength to beat the disease, or ...

He hadn't needed to say more. Georgiana had seen most of the victims of gaol fever die and she knew what the probable outcome would be.

Yet there was a chance. After all, Dinah had survived and now, several weeks after her illness, she'd regained her strength. Georgiana would do everything in her power to ensure Francis survived too.

Once the supplies had been loaded, the master prepared to weigh anchor and take advantage of the westerly winds to sail south to Cape Town — the last stop before Sydney.

Francis was so ill, he was unaware they'd set sail. Time became meaningless to them both. The ship's bell rang out, marking each change of watch but Georgiana was scarcely aware of life outside the cabin.

Even Dinah's appearance with food and fresh water was irregular although Georgiana later discovered that the inconsistent nature of her visits was because she took every opportunity to be with Philip Martin instead of completing the tasks Surgeon Dawson had set her. When the surgeon discovered why she'd taken so long carrying out errands, he'd threatened to inform Captain Yeats who undoubtedly would order the flogging of both midshipman and convict.

Georgiana was unaware of the drama.

Her days and nights were governed by Francis. When he was consumed with fever, she sponged his body with water and moved the sluggish air with the fan he'd bought her in Tenerife. When he fought against whatever demons his hallucinations conjured up, she stroked his head and spoke to him soothingly, and when his body was racked with chills, she piled her blankets on top of his and climbed under them to warm his body with hers. When he slept, she dozed lightly. Surgeon Dawson visited frequently and examined Francis, occasionally bleeding him. The rash had spread from his torso to his limbs and the fever persisted despite Georgiana's attempts to cool him down.

'What more can I do?' she asked.

He shook his head sadly, 'Perhaps you could ask Reverend Leston to say a special prayer for him. Other than that, the outcome's going to depend on Francis' strength.'

Georgiana was reluctant to approach Reverend Leston who she suspected wouldn't be receptive to her plea for a prayer for Francis. Surely God would know her predicament without being told by Reverend Leston? For the first time she acknowledged Francis might die and tears welled up inside her swollen eyelids. When she'd first seen him, shirtless in the hospital with the rash on his back, she'd been sure his youth and strength would beat the disease. But after his slow deterioration, she now had to face the prospect he might soon be gone.

How would she bear it?

When the surgeon had gone, Georgiana studied Francis' face. If he was going to be taken from her, she wanted to remember every detail, but she didn't want to remember him as he was now — skin grey, unshaven, eyes sunken and lips cracked and dry.

Life was so unfair! She longed to see the slow smile which lit up his face and suggested he was just about to reveal a wonderful secret. The way he nibbled his lower lip when he was concentrating and when those deep brown eyes locked with hers as if he could see into her soul.

She knew every part of him, having bathed and cared for him while he was ill. Her body had moulded to his as she'd held him when he'd shivered with cold between bouts of sweating.

Why hadn't it been her who'd caught the fever? She'd willingly give her life so he could live. She wondered if God would allow her to bargain with Him. Would He take her and spare Francis? But she knew He wouldn't. After all, what was her life worth? Very little, it seemed.

* * *

Georgiana had fallen asleep in the chair while sitting by Francis' bedside. She'd leaned forward, resting on the bed and placed her head on her arms. Despite the uncomfortable position, she was fast asleep.

'Georgiana?' Francis said softly, his voice weak and croaky. He'd turned his head towards her and was observing her with a puzzled frown.

Sleep left her immediately because for the first time in many days, he looked as though he was aware of his surroundings which she hoped meant he'd passed the worst of it. She supported his head and held a cup of water to his cracked lips and as he sipped, he closed his eyes in appreciation.

'I think you'll live,' Surgeon Dawson said to Francis when he carried out his next examination, 'but you'll need a lot of care. There could still be complications and you should expect weakness and perhaps depression for some time. But if you continue to improve, there's no reason why you shouldn't be back on duty before we reach Sydney, and knowing you, Francis, possibly even by the time we get to Cape Town. But I'd strongly advise you rest for the next few days at least.'

He caught Georgiana's eye and sent her a silent message which she acknowledged with an almost imperceptible nod of her head. During the earlier outbreak of the fever, he'd told her once the fever had broken and the patient was improving, there was still the possibility of gangrene, kidney or heart failure, coma or even death.

'Concentrate on getting better,' he said, patting Francis' shoulder, and with his usual good humour, added, 'You're doing better than most. I'd given up on you! Your choice of woman was fortunate, indeed. Georgiana hasn't left your side. If it hadn't been for her ... well, only God knows.' He packed his blood-letting instruments in his bag and left.

'You stayed with me the whole time, Georgiana?' Francis asked. His brow was furrowed and he was staring as if he'd never seen her before.

'Of course! You've taken great pains to protect me. The least I could do was to repay the debt.'

'Ah!' he said sadly, 'Yes, duty The things we do to fulfil our duties.'

'I'd have done it anyway,' she said, instantly regretting her words. It was true, but it was better he believed she'd acted out of obligation rather than revealing her feelings for him. She turned her face away from him and started to get up, 'I'll fetch you something to eat.'

But Francis took her wrist and tried to stop her from rising. He was so weak, she could easily have pulled away from his feeble grip but she let him hold her and sat down once again.

'So, it seems I owe you my life ...' he said with that same puzzled expression.

'No! I merely cared for you while your body healed itself.'

'Not merely. I don't recall much, not what you said nor what you did. But I do remember how you made me feel. You comforted me and gave me hope and strength.' He shook his head as if he didn't quite believe his own words, 'Minds can be influenced by circumstances and by other men's beliefs but I'm convinced that souls see the truth. And my soul saw your truth,' he said.

'I'm not sure I understand... '

'And I'm not sure I'm ready to tell you.'

'Hush, you're supposed to be resting.' Had he slipped into delirium again? But his words sounded as though they might be sensible, even if she couldn't understand what they meant.

'And you?' he said, 'You need to rest. I can see by the shadows under your eyes you need sleep. Come,' he pulled gently, 'lay beside me ...' He paused as if trying to recall something on the edge of his memory, 'Yes, I remember. You lay next to me, warming me with your heat ... '

Georgiana climbed beneath the covers. She was tired. No, not tired, she was exhausted.

Perhaps Francis was still slightly delirious despite his fever having broken. He looked at her with genuine fondness. Was he confusing the pretended closeness they'd shown the ship's company with reality? She was too tired to care. How wonderful to lie next to him, wrap her arms around his body and to give herself up to oblivion.

He would remember the truth soon enough.

Francis' recovery was slow. He remained weak, and physical effort left him breathless and exhausted, which in turn frustrated him. 'There are things I need to do!'

Georgiana brought Surgeon Dawson when Francis became agitated but other than prescribing a tonic, he could only shrug. 'The human body recovers in its own time. Rush it and you'll suffer for your foolhardiness,' he said.

To Georgiana's surprise, Francis still treated her as if they had a special friendship. They lay together at night, squashed close in the confines of the bed, their bodies pressed together. During the day, he spoke to her as if she really were his sea-wife; someone he'd chosen, someone he loved. He slept most of the time, and increasingly grew disheartened at his lack of progress.

After one of the surgeon's visits, Georgiana accompanied him back to the hospital so she could ask if it would be possible for someone to carry out inspections of food and water stocks and report back to Francis. She offered to write the records necessary so that at least he would know what was happening on board the ship.

'That might stop him fretting,' Surgeon Dawson said, nodding in approval, 'I'll speak to Captain Yeats.'

Sam Ives, a young sailmaker's mate, was chosen. A short while before, Sam's hands had been crushed beneath a large barrel and while he waited for them to heal, he was told to work for Lieutenant Brooks. Georgiana recorded Sam's reports in Francis' books. But even the effort of directing Sam and Georgiana drained Francis and he grew more despondent.

'You need to be patient,' Georgiana said, growing increasingly alarmed at his desperation.

'I'm as weak as a baby! Even Joseph is surprised at my lack of improvement, although he conceals it. I barely have the strength to sit while you feed me. How much longer will I be like this?'

'I don't know,' she said miserably, 'I could try rubbing your muscles again ...' she faltered when she saw his expression, 'Surgeon Dawson said it might help. If I'm not doing it correctly, I could ask the surgeon again ... I'm sure I'll get it right in the end,' she said.

'There's nothing wrong with the way you did it,' he replied. He sighed and added, 'The problem is, you do it too well.'

'How can that be a problem?'

'Because Georgiana, I am deeply in love with you and your touch awakens something in me I have no energy to pursue. I want to hold you, kiss you and make love to you!'

She gasped, 'Truly?'

'Surely you know ...'

'But our time together has been one of make believe. Convincing others we're lovers.'

Francis sighed, 'Yes, you're right but not any more. And now when I know how much I love you, I can't show you.'

His voice was anguished..

'Oh, but you will, Francis! I love you too and I'll do all I can to make you well.'

He shook his head sadly, 'I may still be in this condition by the time we reach Sydney... '

Neither spoke for a few seconds, imagining what their arrival in New South Wales would bring.

'But that's months away,' Georgiana finally said, 'I'm sure it won't be as bad as you fear.'

* * *

That night, Georgiana hesitated before climbing into bed with Francis, 'If you'd rather I slept on the floor, I understand.'

'No, this is the best part of the day, when I can hold you close. I imagine how it will feel when I can ...' he broke off with a sigh.

Silently, she slipped beneath the blankets and moulded herself to his body. It was important he didn't suspect how desolate she felt.

He'd told her he loved her and expressed a desire to make love to her but despite holding on to Dinah's advice to grab whatever happiness she could, she knew each minute took them closer to Sydney and to their parting. Why was life so cruel? Yet again, it had lured her into believing she might find happiness and then snatched it away. If he regained his strength, they would become lovers but their relationship would be fleeting, over almost before it had begun.

'Are you still awake?' Francis whispered.

'Yes."

'I've been thinking ... Facing death has given me an opportunity to consider my life. I wasted much of my youth, ran up large debts drinking, gambling and... well; I want to be honest with you, Georgiana, I fell in and out of love with the — wrong women, lots of women and now, I don't know what I saw in them. They were all beautiful but shallow, greedy and grasping. There was excitement but not love.'

'Why are you telling me this? I don't need to know about your past.' She didn't want to hear about those women.

'I want to be honest with you because what I feel for you is different. With the others, it was merely physical. Just two people wanting to seize pleasure without any thought of giving. But I love all of you, not just your body... and now, when I want to give you pleasure, I'm unable,' he added sadly. 'But I also want you to understand why this post was so important to me and what I stood to gain on my return home. I was offered a second chance. I have to succeed, to prove to myself I'm not a failure. I don't want to live for the moment. I want a future.'

His words were like a knife twisting in her flesh. *I want a future.* Of course, he did. Wasn't that what anyone wanted?

'I was going to complete this voyage and once I'd proved myself, I planned to find a wife and to settle down... '

She squeezed her eyes tightly shut. Couldn't he see the agony he was inflicting?

'But I didn't realise I'd find love so soon,' he said, 'And now, I have everything I need right here in my arms.'

'Not for much longer... ' she said, swallowing to keep back the tears.

'But that's just it! If I stay in Sydney, we can be together. Once you've served seven years you'll be free. I know that's a long time but we'll be together. I need to get Captain Yeats to release me from my contract. I can't work right now, so I'm no use to him which might go in my favour.'

'You'd give up everything for me? Oh, but Francis! You can't!'

'I'd be giving up nothing of value! I want to be with you more than anything. The question is, do you want a useless man who can barely raise his head off the pillow?'

'More than you can ever know!'

'Then it's settled. When we arrive in Sydney, we'll go ashore together and as soon as possible, we'll be married.'

'You'd marry a criminal?'

'I don't care what you've done in the

past, or what anyone says about you. I've seen the goodness in you. If you'd feigned selflessness all these weeks, at some point, I'd have seen your true character.'

'Since you've shown so much faith and trust in me and shared your past. I feel I must share mine too,' Georgiana said.

'You don't need to speak of your past.'

'It's not that I'm reluctant to tell you anything. I want you to know everything. The reason I'm hesitating is because I vowed to say nothing.'

'Then we won't speak of it again.'

'I'm struggling with my conscience and with another matter,' Georgiana was silent for a few moments; then with a sigh, she asked, 'Do you think it's worse to break an oath to someone than it is to keep secrets from your husband?'

'Only you can decide.'

'But there's a complication. If I tell you, I need your promise to keep my secret ... because someone's life depends on it.'

'This sounds very serious. All I can say is, you can trust me to keep your secrets.'

'As your wife, I'll share everything with you. My reluctance is because if my family discover I've told anyone, my mother may be turned out of her home. I don't think she'd last long in the work-house.'

'Wait! Are you telling me your aunt threatened to hurt your mother if you didn't keep the secret?'

'No, not my aunt, my cousin. And I believe, she'd make it happen.'

'My love, the choice must remain yours but, in my opinion, an oath forced upon you at the expense of your mother's wellbeing sounds like blackmail and I'd argue that an oath made under those conditions was not binding at all.'

Georgiana nodded, 'Then I'll tell you. If we're going to share our lives, I want you to know everything... '

She began by telling him about her father's friend, the artist Gianfranco Mascio, and how her mother had been upset by the miniature he'd painted then about her father's departure.

'I knelt in front of him in the hall, throwing my arms around his knees pleading with him not to go. I might only have been seven years old but I knew this wasn't like any other trip. Even at that young age, I feared I'd never see him again. I think it upset Mama that I begged him to stay because she told him he should take me and her voice was cold. He said she knew that wasn't possible, and I thought it was because he'd be travelling abroad and couldn't take me with him. Mama never spoke of that day again but everything changed. Nothing I did pleased her. It was as if her grief at losing Papa had destroyed her love for me. However much I tried to make amends, her resentment grew.'

'Do you have brothers or sisters — anyone to share the burden?'

'No. I overheard my parents arguing one night and it seems my mother didn't find it easy to bear children, but it's probably for the best. After Papa left, Mama discovered how much money he owed and by the time she'd sold enough to cover the debts, she couldn't afford to keep our house in London. Thankfully, Uncle Thomas offered us a home. I'm not sure he'd have done so if our family had been large.'

'And you never saw your father again?'

'No, never. After we moved into Meadmayne House with Uncle Thomas, everyone spoke about Papa as if he'd died. When I asked Mama about it, she refused to discuss it and merely grew angry. Aunt Alice and Uncle Thomas were evasive and once Mama had suffered her first apoplectic fit, Aunt Alice took me to one side and warned me not to speak of him again. I clung to the hope they were all mistaken but it must have been true. Why else did he not come back to see me? I don't know where he's buried and I never had a chance to say goodbye... ' She wiped a tear away.

'If this is too painful ... '

'No!' she said vehemently, 'I have to tell you everything.' She swallowed and began again, 'Uncle Thomas was good

153

to Mama. She had her own rooms and servants in one of the wings in Mead-mayne House with no worries about money.'

S'That sounds like Thomas — he's one of the most generous men I know. So, you became a sister to his children?'

'No, not a sister. I was companion to Margaret and when John was young, I looked after him. Possibly it would have been better if I'd been a servant. When the thefts were reported, I'd probably have been told to leave, not sentenced to death. One of the servants at Mead-mayne was dismissed for stealing a silver pill box and another for taking Aunt Alice's ring. At the time, I was shocked because neither seemed capable of such a thing. Now I'm almost certain they had no hand in the thefts.'

'So, who?'

'Margaret.'

Francis regarded Georgiana doubt-fully, 'For many reasons, I haven't spent much time with Thomas' family, so I don't know Margaret but she seemed pleasant when I met her years ago.'

'Margaret is charming, beautiful and engaging. So much so, that as we set sail, her marriage to lord Grayford would have taken place.'

'I had an invitation but obviously, couldn't go.'

'Aunt Alice is hoping Lord Grayford's fortune will curb Margaret's unfortunate habit of taking what isn't hers. Aunt believes that once children come along, Margaret will be fully occupied. But I don't think Aunt Alice realises, or perhaps she doesn't want to know, that it's not need that drives Margaret to steal, it's the thrill.'

Francis slowly shook his head as if he couldn't believe her, 'So are you telling me Margaret stole the items you were accused of taking?'

'That's exactly what I'm telling you.'

'But why did you take the blame?'

'Firstly, no one would believe my word against Margaret's, and secondly, she told me she would find a way to discredit Mama and if her parents didn't believe her then when they died, she'd ensure Mama was sent away. Margaret didn't take any chances. She hid several items she'd stolen in my bedroom and ensured they were found. No one doubted my guilt. So I swore to keep Margaret's secret to safeguard my mother. I had no idea I'd be prosecuted but Margaret had taken a watch from a shop and the watchmaker pressed charges, so there was no question of returning it and paying him for any inconvenience. He wanted to make an example of the thief, so it was made public and the more public it became, the more the Tilcott family had to distance themselves from me.'

'My God, Georgiana! This is monstrous! I can't believe this is the same man we both know.'

'He was trying to protect his family.'

'You're part of his family!'

'But not his immediate family. At least he spoke to the judge on my behalf and instead of hanging, I was reprieved. And he engaged you to look after me on the voyage. If he hadn't, I'd never have met you, so I am forever in his debt!'

'I don't know how you can be so calm about it.'

'I have no choice. At first, I intended to end my life once we'd put to sea. I was going to throw myself overboard although whether I'd have had the courage to do it, I don't know. Before it came to that, you rescued me. Then, when I knew I could survive the voyage, I decided I'd work hard in Sydney, endure whatever life threw at me for seven years and then return to England. But now, I have you and my life's changed completely!'

'I thought Thomas was an honourable man. It's hard to believe he could allow this to happen. Was it possible he didn't know about Margaret?'

'He knew. But don't think badly of him. It was a choice between his beloved daughter and me. He had to protect Margaret and I was the price.'

'I don't think in your place I'd be so generous,' Francis said and kissed her temple. He breathed in sharply, making her jump.

'What is it? Are you in pain? Shall I fetch Surgeon Dawson?'

Francis smiled, 'No, my love! I just had a wonderful idea! It surprised me I hadn't thought of it before. Why wait until we reach Sydney to marry? I'll see Captain Yeats tomorrow to tell him I want to leave the ship in Sydney and ask him for permission to marry as soon as we get to Cape Town in a few days.'

'Oh, Francis, I don't think I've ever been happier in my life!'

★ ★ ★

Francis' strength gradually began to return and shortly before the ship was due to reach Cape Town, he went to see Captain Yeats to ask for permission to leave the ship's company in Sydney and to marry Georgiana as soon as possible. The captain wasn't happy about losing Francis but said he wouldn't stand in his way and gave his permission for the marriage to go ahead although he'd strongly suggested Francis reconsider his rash decision, even suggesting the gaol fever had addled his wits!

Francis returned to Georgiana to give her the good news that they'd be married as soon as the ship arrived in Cape Town.

She flew to his arms, 'Oh, Francis! I'm so happy! I didn't think I'd ever be able to say that again! I can't believe we'll soon be man and wife.'

Francis held her tightly, laying his cheek against her head, then with a deep sigh, he pushed her gently away.

'Francis?' Georgiana said, blood draining from her face as she saw his agonised expression. 'What's wrong? Have you changed your mind?'

'No, sweetheart!' he said, pulling her to him again, 'I swear no one will make me give you up ... if you still want me.'

'Of course, I want you! How can you even ask?'

'You said we'll be man and wife, and legally, that will be so, but ...' He looked away from her and stared into the distance, 'I'm exhausted after my short walk to see the master... It may take a while before we'll truly be man and wife.'

'You're improving each day. Not long ago, you could barely stand. But that doesn't matter to me! In time, your strength will return fully and then,' she nuzzled into his neck, 'And then, my love, we'll make up for lost time! Now, you must rest.'

'I want to write to Thomas first. I need to explain why I won't be returning to England. I'm not sure where I stand with him now. He paid my debts before I left on condition I made this journey and looked after you. I'll definitely be looking after you — in fact, for the rest of my life — but I won't be completing the journey. So, I don't know if he'll consider I carried out my side of the bargain.'

'I wonder how he'll take the news. He'll surely assume I'll tell you about Margaret, but if we're both settled in Sydney, the secret will remain there. And if Margaret makes a success of her marriage, then everyone will be happy.'

'I can't believe your generosity, Georgiana,' he said, his face radiant with love.

'Sit,' she said, embarrassed by his praise, 'Give your muscles a chance to rest. I'll get your writing box and you can tell me what to write.'

'My dear Thomas,' Francis began and Georgiana dipped the quill in the ink, scraped the excess off and after writing down his words, she nodded for him to continue.

'I hope this letter finds you, my sister, Margaret and John well.'

Georgiana tipped her head to one side and regarded him with surprise, 'Shouldn't you mention Aunt Alice in that list?'

'I have.'

'Ah, yes, I see. You mean my sister-in-law.'

'No,' he said, surprised, 'Alice is my sister.'

Georgiana dropped the pen making an ink splash in the middle of the paper, 'How can that be? Aunt Alice can't be your sister!'

'I know there's an age gap but I assure you she is. I was what our mother called a late blessing. My elder sister, Cecile was married before I was born and Alice married when I was young. I joined the Navy early, so I don't really know either of my sisters.'

'Oh God!' moaned Georgiana, 'Please tell me that's not true!' She stood abruptly, the chair tipping backwards and falling with a crash.

'Georgiana! What's wrong? Tell me!'

'My God, Francis! If Alice and Cecile are your sisters ... ' she held her hands to her mouth and stared in horror, her eyes wide and tear filled. 'Cecile is my mother. That makes you my uncle!'

'But I thought you were the daughter of one of Thomas' sisters!'

'And I thought you were related to Thomas too! I had no idea you were my mother's brother.'

'My God! What have we done?'

'Nothing! We've done nothing! Except fall in love where we shouldn't have. Can we be blamed for that?'

'I don't know! How could this have happened?'

'I'll go back to the prison quarters,' Georgiana said picking up her blankets.

'No! I promised Thomas I'd look after you until we reached Sydney and I'll do that. We managed before ...' He swallowed, 'I mean we managed at the beginning of the voyage, we'll continue like that. You won't be welcomed back onto the prison deck. I'll sleep on the floor and you can have the bed. We'll just wind the clock back as if we'd never loved and ... Oh, please don't cry, Georgiana, I can't bear it.'

★ ★ ★

Captain Yeats was pleased to learn Francis had changed his mind and would sail with the ship to Canton and if he doubted Francis' explanation that he had, in fact, not been in his right mind before, he didn't show it.

Georgiana worked with Surgeon Dawson in the hospital helping to treat many of the sailors who were suffering from scurvy. There'd been another outbreak of the bloody flux among the prisoners and several cases of pneumonia. He was grateful for the help and Georgiana was relieved to immerse herself in something which kept her from her bed until exhaustion overtook her.

Francis had not completely recovered, but he too, was driving himself to extreme fatigue.

When the ship arrived in Cape Town, Georgiana remained with Surgeon Dawson, while Francis spent time ashore, supervising the purchase and loading of supplies.

Finally, the stores were safely aboard and the captain gave the order to prepare to leave on the morrow. With favourable conditions, in eighty days, the Lady Amelia would sail into Sydney Cove and convey all the convicts ashore. After restocking, all haste would be made to set sail to China. And Francis would be able to begin to forget his... he dared not say the word love because anything he felt for Georgiana had been wicked and grotesque.

She was his niece. No, he would forget everything which had happened aboard the Lady Amelia between Rio de Janeiro and Cape Town. After all, he'd been gravely ill and if he tried hard, he could almost pretend everything had been one long hallucination. He would never think about it again. And he would never, ever speak of it.

4

The Lady Amelia sailed out of Table Bay, heading into the westerly winds towards the notorious latitudes between 40 and 50 degrees south of the equator which sailors referred to as the Roaring Forties. Two days after her departure, the merchant ship, Emerald, sailed into Table Bay.

The Emerald had left Portsmouth several weeks after the Lady Amelia but she'd sailed directly to Cape Town and if she hadn't encountered violent storms which had damaged her mainmast and rigging, she'd have arrived much sooner and the letters she carried for Captain Yeats, his crew and several of the convicts would have been delivered. The Emerald's master understood how disappointed people on the Lady Amelia would be when they realised their mail had missed them by two days but it couldn't be helped. Once the Emerald was provisioned, she too would sail to Sydney Cove with her cargo of food, livestock and clothing. Letters would be delivered then. If the wind and tides were against the Emerald, well, she was a speedy ship and would undoubtedly catch the Lady Amelia by the time she reached China. There was nothing the master could do about it and knew Edgar Yeats of the Lady Amelia would understand.

Onboard the Emerald among the post, was a letter addressed to Miss Georgiana Aylwood. It was from her mother, Cecile who'd written it not long after Georgiana had sailed on the Lady Amelia.

When Cecile's daughter had admitted she'd stolen a watch and other expensive items, Cecile had been deeply ashamed because people would hold her responsible for Georgiana's immorality and failings. If she'd known it would come to this, she'd have revealed the truth. But how could she have known? The girl took after the deceitful father whose looks she had inherited.

Even now, when Cecile thought of Joshua, she felt her stomach twist and her heart pound. The passing years had not diminished her hatred of the man who'd betrayed her. Sometimes in the middle of the night, she woke and wondered if he really was dead as she wanted to believe. At least, he'd only attempted to see her once but Thomas had threatened to set the dogs on him and he'd never returned.

Cecile had suffered for so long, she'd grown accustomed to her disabilities. Alice ensured she was cared for and needed for nothing. But during the last few weeks, Cecile's heart had begun to behave most strangely. At times it raced, at others it seemed to flap like a fish out of water, and afterwards, she felt exhausted. She'd told no one. Dr Jefferson was a fool and would simply drain more blood from her. Anyway, she suspected — no, she knew — she was dying. Death held no fears. She'd been marking time for years. But during the last week, when she'd woken in the small hours, it occurred to her she needed to make the truth known before it was too late. She must make it clear that Georgiana was nothing to do with her and therefore not her failure. And if there was a chance that Joshua was still alive, she needed everyone to know how he'd mistreated her.

The sooner she committed her words to paper, the better. She'd already made enquiries and it appeared that a merchant ship called the Emerald would be leaving England shortly, heading for New South Wales. The girl would be there for seven years and it didn't matter when she finally read it, so long as she eventually knew the truth ...

Georgiana,

By the time you read this letter, I expect I will have gone to my Maker. I have been suffering with my heart for some time; not entirely unexpected after your wicked behaviour. People have offered their sympathy and condolences at having raised such a dishonest, ungrateful daughter. They pity me. But as you will see, their pity is wasted.

I prayed for years that I would bear a child but God did not see fit to answer my pleas. One day when your father returned from Europe, he arrived with a newborn baby. He had caught a chill on his way home from Portsmouth and had stayed a few nights at an inn. While he was there, the innkeeper's daughter died in childbirth. Your father said the wretched man begged him to take the child as he was a widower and could not care for it. So, your father brought her home and suggested we raise her as our own. I was so desperate for a child, I agreed. Since we had just moved to London from Dorset, we knew none of our neighbours and we were able to pass you off as our own child. Neither had I seen Alice for some time and I simply told her I had not realised I was with child until many months had passed.

I believed we had given a poor, unfortunate baby who might otherwise have gone to the workhouse, a loving home and a good upbringing. What I hadn't realised was that your father had lied. He had been travelling in Europe with his mistress who had given birth to his child. It was she who had died. The baby your father brought home for me to raise as my own, was you.

Why I didn't see the likeness between you two before, I have no idea. It took Gianfranco to point out what was so obvious. Your dark, curly hair and your eyes were so similar to your father's, it could not have been chance. And it wasn't chance. Your father finally confessed. Then, like the coward he was, he walked out leaving all his debts to me.

What happened after that, you already know.

Over the years, I have been reminded of a cuckoo leaving its egg in another bird's nest and then flying off. Of course, it is not the cuckoo chick's fault and I freely acknowledge you were not the guilty party. That honour belongs to your father. When I discovered your origins, I could have turned you out of my house but I did not. I tried to do my Christian duty and bring you up to respect the law so when I learned of your crimes, I was truly shocked and bitterly regretted my charity towards you. Therefore, before it is too late, I am telling you this to let you know that I disown you. You are no part of me.

One further point. When I die, I leave you nothing in my will. If you had remained obedient, I might have found it in my heart to leave you something but you have proved to be greedy and dishonest. May God have mercy on you.

Cecile Aylwood.

Cecile sprinkled sand on the letter and when the ink had dried, addressed it to Georgiana. She took a sip of her laudanum medicine, grimaced at its bitter taste and called her maid. It would be many months before the girl read the letter, by which time Cecile would be free of pain and in the family crypt in the church. She sealed and pressed her signet ring into the molten wax, then instructed the maid to ensure the captain of the Emerald received the letter before he set sail ...

After much deliberation, she smoothed a fresh sheet of paper in front of her and prepared to write to her sister, Alice. She was grateful to her for taking her in and it seemed only right to tell her the truth. Once she was gone, it wouldn't matter if her sister, who'd managed to produce two fine children, knew how she'd been barren and then duped by her adulterous husband into raising a child who wasn't hers. And it was best she understood why she didn't intend to leave any money to the girl she'd once believed was her daughter.

Later, the maid found Cecile slumped over her desk with the finished letter to Alice addressed and sealed in front of her.

She had died alone.

*   *   *

The captain of the Emerald was keen to set sail. Conditions were perfect and there were sufficient provisions aboard to last until Sydney Cove. However, the day before they were due to depart, the carpenter allowed a pot of pitch to boil over, starting a fire on the main deck which was only brought under control after the mainsail had been badly damaged.

It was several days before the Emerald was ready to weigh anchor, by which time, the Lady Amelia had gained a considerable lead and was being battered by ferocious weather as she made her way through the notorious Roaring Forties. The treacherous westerly winds typical of this part of the Southern Ocean brought strong gales and mountainous seas with waves which crashed over the decks. Water gushed below and streamed through gaps in ill-sealed timbers, ensuring everyone and everything was drenched.

To increase the hardship of all those aboard the Lady Amelia, it was bitterly cold in the sub Antarctic and news that the southwest of Van Diemen's Land had been sighted was eagerly received.

Georgiana, wrapped in two shawls, looked out from the main deck at the distant land with its snow-topped hills and the pinpricks of native fires here and there, and wondered if Sydney was like this, cold and unwelcoming. Not that it mattered.

Ever since she'd discovered the blood link to Francis, her heart had felt as numb as her fingers which clutched the rail. When she'd been sentenced in court, it had seemed inconceivable that Fate could punish her more severely. And yet, it had thrust a man upon her whom she'd come to love. But not just any man. No, he was her uncle, a man forbidden to her. And a man with whom she would have committed a grave sin had circumstances been different and had he recovered from his illness sooner. Not only that, but Fate had not snatched Francis completely away, giving her a chance to heal. No, it had forced the two of them to see each other daily and be within reach each night, so the terrible wound in her heart couldn't begin to heal. She pulled the shawls tighter around her with frozen, unbending fingers and turned back to the cabin, knowing the feeling in her hands would return which was more than could be said for her heart.

* * *

Ten days later, the wind moved to the south west, blowing a breeze that had been warmed over the land, towards the Lady Amelia as it approached the south and north heads of Port Jackson, the inlet leading to Sydney Cove.

Georgiana gazed at the wild, untamed landscape. The endless blue skies looked down on sandstone outcrops and slopes thickly covered in trees that grew down to the water's edge, the dense growth interspersed with yellow sand. Although rocks, forests and beaches were all found in England, somehow, these were completely foreign. Perhaps it was the dazzling sunlight shining with an intensity that hurt the eyes. Or the strange calls of the birds wheeling overhead or more likely, the occasional glimpse of a black figure standing on a beach holding a spear which in the blink of an eye was reabsorbed into the dense forest as if it had been a shadow.

Georgiana shuddered. The future loomed dark and brooding; filled with known horrors such as Arthur Towler and unknown terrors which she couldn't begin to guess at.

Cutting through the usual shipboard sounds, the creaking, flapping and rattling, she distinguished Francis' deep, throaty laugh but she didn't turn around. Miss Chesterton's high pitched whinny could also be heard and Georgiana didn't want to see them together. She didn't want to see Francis at all, it was too painful and too shocking to think of the taboo they might have broken. At least once he'd sailed, she'd be able to … what? Forget him? No! She could never do that. But she would lock his memory away in the furthest reaches of her mind.

As the Lady Amelia glided into the

cove, Georgiana saw a stream which divided Sydney in two. Open land to the east, and rockier, hilly land to the west. People stood on the wharf waving and shouting at the newly-arrived ship.

'They can't wait to get their 'ands on the supplies we brought 'em,' a sailor observed as he paused from his work to look at the inhabitants of Sydney, 'Ive heard they're 'alf starved.' Then, presumably remembering that Georgiana would soon join the people on shore, he added more kindly, 'But that were a while ago. They might 'ave 'ad better luck with their crops since then.'

* * *

Captain Yeats, several officers including Francis, and the passengers went ashore to meet Governor Arthur Phillip who'd sailed with the First Fleet of convicts to arrive in New South Wales in 1788.

It was Georgiana's final night in Francis' cabin and the following morning, the women and their belongings were to be conveyed ashore by longboat. Indeed, it was possible she wouldn't see Francis even to speak to again.

She barely slept that night, listening to the water slapping against the hull and to the strange calls of the nocturnal animals on land. She pretended to be asleep when Francis and the others came aboard much later. Outside the cabin, Miss Chesterton's annoying laughter rang out in response to something Francis said and Georgiana heard sufficient to know they were discussing China. There was no doubt Miss Chesterton had Francis in her sights and during the long journey to Canton, Georgiana thought she'd try her utmost to wear down his resistance. Perhaps it was for the best. Georgiana couldn't begrudge him female company, even if it was Miss Chesterton.

She woke at four o'clock and watched as the dawn light streaked through the salt-encrusted window pane. Francis had already risen and left the cabin. She had wondered if they would say good-bye. Now she had her answer. As she washed and dressed for the last time in the cabin, she felt torn he'd left without saying anything — sad the time had come to part and relieved not to endure the pain of their final farewell.

$$\star \quad \star \quad \star$$

To Georgiana's dismay, she was allocated to the same longboat as the red-headed convict, Mary Norris, who'd become well-known for her bad temper and flying fists. 'Look! It's the Duchess!' she said when she saw Georgiana climb into the boat, 'not so 'igh and mighty now, is she?'

The other women laughed and moved so there was no room for Georgiana, until one of the sailors roughly shoved them aside to make a place. Her chest was tossed in on top of the other boxes and the sailors cast off from the Lady Amelia.

Georgiana lowered her head, avoiding eye contact with the occupants of the boat to deter more taunts. She tried to focus on the pool of water in the keel which slopped back and forth, and not look back at the ship for a glimpse of Francis. But the temptation was too great and she couldn't resist glancing up at the deck.

Her stomach knotted when she saw someone leaning over the side of the ship staring at her.

It wasn't Francis. It was Arthur Towler. He licked his flabby lips, then with a sneer, he formed them into the word You. The threat was clear and with a sharp intake of breath, she looked down into the keel, feeling queasy and trying to block the memory of the abhorrent face.

'Looks like you've already caught yerself another man, Duchess,' Mary. said, having witnessed the silent exchange between Georgiana and Towler. She shook her head in mock dismay, 'Tut tut! Hardly out of one bed and you're slippin' into the next.'

Georgiana ignored her but the others joined in: 'Why don't you shut up!' a sailor said.

'What's it to you?' Mary asked, her fists bunched ready for a fight.

'I've 'ad enough of you and yer cronies to last me a lifetime. I can't wait till all you women are off the ship and we can 'ave a bit of peace an' quiet. Always screaming about sommat. Always causin' trouble.'

Mary spent the rest of the journey to the wharf aiming barbed comments at the sailor who told her he was going to make her regret her words as soon as they were ashore and the other women laughed at Mary's observations about the sailor's appearance and were excited at the prospect of a fight. Georgiana continued to study the dirty water which sloshed back and forth in the keel, as the longboat rode the waves, grateful to the sailor who'd distracted Mary from tormenting her.

Once ashore, the women were lined up while the marine officer warned them to keep to their part of the camp. He told them where to get rations and water, and ordered them to reassemble at 6pm on the parade ground when Governor Phillip would address the entire assembly.

'Follow him,' he said to the first four women in the line who filed after a marine towards the huts of the women's camp.

Mary Norris was at the end of the line and would be first to be chosen for the next hut and there were four women between her and Georgiana. If each hut held four women, Georgiana would not be selected to sleep in the same hut as Mary but before the officer could indicate the next four women to be escorted to their new borne, the convict next to Georgiana fainted, her knees buckling and her body slumping forward.

The officer looked at her in annoyance as if she'd deliberately interrupted his task and curtly ordered one of his men to take her to the hospital.

'You, you, you and you. Follow him,' he said to the women with a jerk of his head and Georgiana, Mary and two of her friends accompanied the young marine.

'And what's your name?' Mary asked the man, slipping her arm through his as soon as they were out of sight of the officer. His cheeks burned bright red but he seemed pleased at the attention and told her he was Private James Long. 'Well, Private Long, it's nice to know there's a friendly face on this godforsaken place. And yours is such an 'andsome one,' Mary said in silky tones. Private Long's cheeks glowed even more but he didn't try to remove Mary's arm. 'So, if there's anything I can do for you ...' Mary smiled at him and the young marine almost choked with embarrassment.

'H ... here,' he said stopping at one of the huts, 'this is where I'm supposed to take you.'

'Aren't you going to take us in and show us around?' Mary asked looking through her eyelashes at him.

'Private Long!' An officer yelled, spotting the young man's predicament, 'Get back to the parade ground!'

'Yes sir!' The crimson-cheeked marine disengaged his arm and hurried away to the laughter of the three women.

Mary pushed open the ill-fitting door and peered into the gloomy interior of their new home. A combination of humidity and extreme heat had resulted in the timber twisting and splitting, leaving different sized gaps in the walls, one of which became an exit for a rat who, disturbed by the presence of the woman at the door, ran across the floor and disappeared.

A group of male convicts carried the women's baggage to the middle of the camp and after piling it in a heap, they were ordered to leave by the accompanying marines, in an obvious attempt to keep the two sexes apart. With so many new female arrivals, the convicts and marines alike were reluctant to go and the officer in charge became increasingly flustered as he urged his men to move faster and ignore the women.

Mary and the other two convicts, Sadie and Ann, helped each other carry their belongings into the hut but left Georgiana to drag her chest on her own and by the time she'd pulled it across the dusty earth, the other women had taken the best places, leaving her space near the door.

It was clear Mary considered herself in charge. 'Ann and Sadie, light the fire. Duchess and I will go and fetch our rations and water,' she told them and walked out of the hut as if she knew her orders would be obeyed.

Georgiana considered her. Since she'd come ashore, it was as if her mind and body had become disengaged from reality. Before, she'd been afraid but now, if she refused to acknowledge fear, it couldn't hurt her. After all, what more could Fate throw at her? She should have been in the hut next door with three different women but Fate had decreed she'd be thrown together with the woman who was most antagonistic towards her and two others who'd do anything to avoid trouble. If Georgiana could detach herself from her feelings, then even Mary with her sharp tongue and quick fists had no power over her. She would be derided and probably attacked but if she'd made up her mind not to recognise the pain, then it couldn't hurt her.

'Well, are you coming, Duchess?' Mary asked, her eyebrows drawn slightly together as if puzzled that anyone should dare to do other than her bidding. Ann and Sadie stopped what they were doing, waiting to see what would happen but Georgiana merely nodded and followed Mary outside. After all, they needed food and water, so she might as well help.

'This ain't the sort of life you're used to, eh?' Mary said.

Georgiana shook her head. She didn't want to talk about what she'd been used to with this woman who was undoubtedly probing for details she could share with Ann and Sadie later so they could ridicule her.

'It's the sort of life I'm used to though. Don't suppose you know what it's like to be poor.'

Georgiana remained silent. There would be a point to this one sided conversation, she knew. Mary wasn't the sort of woman to idly gossip and her friendliness was completely uncharacteristic.

'I 'spect you can read an' write though, eh?' Mary said. Georgiana nodded. 'Not very chatty, are you?'

Georgiana sighed. 'I have very little to say.'

The two women walked on in silence, then Mary said, 'So, if someone were to ask you to write something for them, what would you want in return?'

'Nothing,' said Georgiana, in surprise, 'I'd Simply write it.'

'No one does somethin' fer nothin'! Kathleen Findlay's sister, Betsy, has been in Sydney since the First Fleet arrived and she said one of the convicts'll write a letter for you if you keep buying him drinks. But he won't start until he's 'ad a few and you got to make sure he's finished before he's 'ad so many he falls off 'is stool.'

'Well, if you want me to write something for you, I'd be happy to do it.'

'There's more to it than that,' Mary

said, looking right and left to make sure no one could overhear. 'It's just that I like to keep my private life to meself ... '

'I see. And presumably you wouldn't want the contents of your letter to be spoken about.'

'I can see you and me understand each other. So, when can you do it fer me? I want me letter to go with the Lady Amelia when it leaves.'

'If there's enough light, I'll do it tonight.'

'Not in the hut, I don't want the other two knowing my business.'

'Then we'll find somewhere quiet.'

★ ★ ★

On arriving back at the hut with the rations and the water pitchers, they entered to see the contents of Georgiana's chest strewn over the dusty ground. Ann was holding Georgiana's petticoats. against her and waving the fan Francis had bought in Tenerife. Sadie, wearing Georgiana's bonnet, curtseyed, saying,

189

'Yes, your Duchessness! How lovely, your Duchessness!'

Both women looked towards Mary, expecting her approval. When she didn't join in the laughter, they froze, uncertain whether to continue.

Mary put the pitchers down and grabbed Ann, who was nearest, pushing her face close, she said, 'You don't touch anything that belongs to the Duchess! Is that clear?'

'We was just —'

'I don't care what you was just doin', I'm tellin' you not to touch her things. Now fold it all up and put it back.'

Sadie backed away from Mary's reach and after removing the bonnet she threw it in the chest.

'Careful!' Mary yelled at her.

With a cry of dismay, Georgiana stooped to pick up her writing box which had been turned out of the chest and was upside down on the ground with the contents strewn around. Mary seized Ann's neckerchief with both fists and pushed her face so close, their noses were almost touching, 'If anything's broken, I'll break you!'

'It's all fine,' said Georgiana, not wanting trouble. Then she had an idea, 'Some of the ink has spilled, so I'll take it down to the stream to wash.' She gave Mary a meaningful look.

'I'll pour you a basin of water,' Ann said in a wheedling voice.

Following Georgiana's train of thought, Mary said, 'Keep yer basin! The Duchess said she's goin' to the stream. By the time we get back, you'll have folded all 'er things and put them back.'

As Georgiana left the hut with her writing box under her arm, she looked back to see Ann and Sadie whispering together, their faces full of anger and resentment — she'd just made more enemies. But Mary, the most aggressive of them all, would have to be pleasant to her, at least until the letter was written. Georgiana realised that once she knew the contents of the letter, she would be privy to Mary's 'business', whatever that was. Mary would surely be aware that if

191

she upset Georgiana, her secret might not be safe.

Perhaps life in the camp wasn't going to be as hard as it had first appeared. Although Francis had said he would ask the governor to make provision for her, she was still being treated the same as everyone else. Presumably Francis' request had been denied, if indeed, he'd had a chance to make one.

The two women found a quiet place to sit by the stream and Mary told Georgiana what she wanted written. The letter was to her two daughters who were living with their grandmother in St Giles, a notorious London slum. The girls' father had long gone and Mary had been the breadwinner of the family, earning her money walking the streets. One day she'd dipped into a wealthy client's pocket and helped herself to his cash. It had been a large sum and had earned her the death sentence which had been commuted to transportation. Now, she was worried about how her mother would cope with two small girls and she wanted her daughters to have a letter to remind them of her, even if they wouldn't be able to read it.

'There won't be money to spare to get someone to read it to 'em but you never know, one day my girls might learn to read ... if they don't starve to death first. But I'm goin' to do everything I can to send 'em money, if I have to put up with every man in Sydney.'

'There are other ways of earning money.'

'Fer the likes o' you, Duchess, there may be. But fer me...? Anyway,' she added with a toss of her red mane, 'I don't care. I might even prefer to earn my money like that. It's easy, see.'

Georgiana had spent enough time with Mary to know she was bluffing and enough time with the women onboard the Lady Amelia who'd plied their trade among the sailors to know it was a hard and unhealthy way to earn a living.

Georgiana could see that Mary's method of survival was to lash out first before anyone had a chance to hit her, thereby maintaining her reputation as a fiery and dangerous opponent. It had worked so far since no one had the courage to stand up to her. But if the others knew she was anxious about her mother and daughters, she believed it would undermine her notoriety.

When the letter was finished and the ink had dried, the two women made their way back to the hut. Mary said in her usual brash tones, 'If you think you're going to use that information against me, Duchess, be very careful. I won't hesitated to stick a knife in you. I've got nothing to lose, see. Nothing to lose at all.'

* * *

At ten to six, the women assembled on the marines' parade ground waiting for Governor Phillip to speak to them. He arrived promptly at six, dressed in full uniform with his British and Portuguese awards on his breast. After removing his bicorne hat, he spoke eloquently of his vision for the settlement at Sydney Cove, warning that crimes would be dealt with most harshly, especially the theft of food from anyone, convict or freeman, which was punishable by hanging. He encouraged the women to work hard to ensure all the inhabitants of Sydney prospered and finished by warning them it was forbidden for men to enter the women's camp after dark and that soldiers had been ordered to fire at anyone caught attempting to do so. It was therefore unwise for women to invite men to enter. The punishment for infringement of other laws was flogging, and he looked meaningfully at the steel triangle at the side of the parade ground to which those found guilty would be strapped.

By the time he'd finished, dark storm clouds had gathered overhead and out at sea thunder rumbled and lightning zigzagged across the sky. The governor finished his speech, settled his hat firmly on his head and, accompanied by his clerk, strode away, hands clasped behind his back.

A captain stepped forward and instructed the women whose names he would call out to remain behind, while the other women were to return directly to their camp. A list of names was called out, including Georgiana's and Dinah's.

'Aylwood and Trevithick, report to the governor's residence tomorrow at eight. You two return to your huts,' he told Georgiana and Dinah.

As Georgiana hurried through the camp, enormous drops of rain splattered around her, battering the thatched roofs of the huts. Across the stream on the eastern side of Sydney, far off in the forest, lightning struck and the deafening clap of thunder overhead shook the ground. She noticed her pallet had been moved further into the hut than it had been when the women had first claimed the best places and assumed it was Mary who'd persuaded the other two to give up some of their space.

No one slept well that night. The storm crashed overhead for hours and once it had passed, the night was filled with strange animal sounds and the voices of women who'd defied the nightly curfew. And then, inside the hut was the rustling of unidentified animals and the torment of huge, biting ants.

As Georgiana washed and dressed in the morning, her eyelids were puffy and heavy with lack of sleep and her legs bore the marks of the ants which had nipped her during the night. Dinah was waiting for her at the edge of the women's camp and her eyes were sunken as though she'd had a bad night too.

'Why d'you think they picked us out to see the governor?' Dinah asked, 'D'you think they'll want us to work in the hospital?'

Most of the other women in the camp had been assigned duties the previous evening. About half of them would be sewing clothes and the rest would be working in the fields. Many would be sent to private farms and businesses which had begun to establish themselves in and around Sydney as well as nearby Parramatta where the soil was richer and more suited to farming.

Georgiana wouldn't have minded sewing but working in the fields in the heat of the day didn't appeal and having worked with Surgeon Dawson, she and Dinah had learned much about diseases and remedies. They'd be more help as nurses.

Thankfully, that was indeed Governor Phillip's intention. Dinah and Georgiana were ushered into his office by the clerk, who introduced them and after looking them up and down, Governor Phillip consulted his books.

'Captain Yeats and Lieutenant Brooks recommended that these two convicts should be sent to work with the surgeon-general, your excellency,' the clerk said.

'I see. I trust you're amenable to this?' he asked, scrutinising both women again.

'Yes, sir! Thank you, sir!'

The clerk slid the paper to him and he signed it. 'Is there anyone else to see, Mr Brewer?'

'No, your excellency but I believe we

still have to find a washerwoman ... '

'Ah, yes indeed, thank you, Mr Brewer.'

He turned back to Georgiana and Dinah, 'Would either of you ladies know of anyone who isn't afraid of hard work nor of some of the sights and sounds you know are part of hospital life? Surgeon White has need of a washerwoman. But the last three women assigned to the job spent much of their time either fainting or vomiting. Not a pleasant job I'm sure but there must be someone among you who's up to the task.'

'I believe I may know of someone, sir,' Georgiana said.

Dinah looked sideways at her.

'Yes?' said the governor, 'And her name?'

'Mary Norris, sir.'

Dinah gasped and looked at Georgiana but neither of the men noticed.

'Have you got that name, Mr Brewer?'

The clerk nodded, 'Yes, your excellency. I'll send a man to fetch her now.'

'Thank you, that will be all,' Governor Phillip said to the two women, waving them away before adding, 'Your belongings will be brought to the hut where the nurses live. A finer place than your current homes, I think you'll find.'

'Have you taken leave o' yer senses?' Dinah asked when they were outside, 'Mary Norris?'

'Possibly,' Georgiana said.

She was unsure if she'd done the right thing. She knew that Mary had said she didn't mind how she earned money to send back to her daughters, but washing hospital linen was not going to be pleasant, even if the accommodation was promised to be better.

Then there was the possibility that Mary would lose her temper and start a fight, in which case it wouldn't go well for Georgiana, who'd recommended her.

* * *

Their new home was brick-built and much sturdier than the ramshackle timber huts of the women's camp and much more comfortable, as Governor Phillip had said, but the work wasn't quite as they'd experienced aboard the ship.

During the voyage, there'd been one stabbing during a drunken brawl but the attacker's aim had been impaired by rum and the victim had merely been slashed in the arm. Surgeon Dawes had sewn it up and, other than leaving a scar, the arm had been as good as new.

However, in Surgeon White's hospital, patients died in agony from snake bites, and others from spear wounds after having been ambushed by the natives — some of them being carried back to camp by friends, still with the spear protruding from their bodies.

Alongside the convicts and freemen who'd arrived in Sydney during the last few years, there were the natives — or Aborigines as Governor Phillip referred to them — the people who had been living on the land from the beginning, dark skinned people, who preferred to go naked, showing their profusion of ritual scars, long cuts on their shoulders, chests or bellies. Gracie Lloyd, one of the nurses who'd shown the two women what to do, had explained that each scar had its own meaning, such as whether boys or girls had reached adulthood.

'They knock out one of the front teeth of the boys in a ceremony, too,' she told them, 'That's why they so readily accept Governor Phillip, because he's got a front tooth missing and they think he's been initiated like them.'

The work was sometimes sickening and often distressing but Georgiana set about learning all she could from Surgeon White who'd been studying native plants and their medicinal properties since he'd arrived with the First Fleet.

Mary had taken the job as washerwoman and although she hadn't said so, Georgiana knew she was grateful her name had been put forward for the job. Although Georgiana had worried Mary's temper might lose her the job, she was working twice as hard as necessary and taking in washing to make a few pennies extra. She was offensive and unpleasant to everyone as she'd always been and probably would continue to be, while she felt she had to protect herself, and she was still nasty to Georgiana who understood the harsh words were necessary to maintain Mary's reputation and not because she meant them.

On the day the lady Amelia sailed out of Sydney Cove, Georgiana kept busy in the hospital. Surgeon White's assistant, David Oakley, was operating on a man with a gangrenous foot and she volunteered to assist him. Dinah went to the shore to wave goodbye to the ship — and to Philip Martin, the midshipman who hadn't fulfilled his promise to stay in Sydney and marry her and be a father to the child she was carrying.

''E'll come back,' she said to Georgiana, 'After 'e's got enough saved for a place for the baby an' me. 'E'll come back.'

Georgiana wondered if she really believed it but she understood why Dinah wanted to go to wave him off in case he changed his mind. Gracie had been seeing one of the lady Amelia's sailors and had also gone to wave farewell to her man.

'Well, thank goodness we've got one nurse who knows her priorities,' Surgeon Oakley said.

Georgiana smiled politely. To have watched the Lady Amelia sail away would have felt as though her heart were being ripped out of her chest.

She wondered if Francis would stand on deck waving with the other crew members. Probably not. It wasn't that she thought he'd have forgotten her, that was most unlikely. They'd shared something so intense she almost felt like they were one being. No, the problem was that he would want to forget her, would actively be crowding the memory of her from his mind, erasing it as if she had never been. What else could he do? The shame of what had almost taken place needed to be buried and forgotten. And she knew that as the uncle, he'd assumed most of the guilt despite the fact there were only a few years difference between them.

'Aylwood? Aylwood! If you can't concentrate, you might as well leave me to do this myself!' Surgeon Oakley snapped.

★   ★   ★

The day after the Lady Amelia glided out of Sydney Cove and set sail for Canton, the look-out on the southern head at the entrance to Port Jackson signalled that he'd spotted a ship and shortly after, the Emerald hove into view.

The letters it carried for Governor Phillip, various officials and officers were delivered to the governor's residence and were eagerly opened and the news from home —, already months out of date — was read and reread, then discussed.

The letter addressed to Georgiana Aylwood was delivered the following day to the hut where the nurses lived.

Her heart leapt when she was given the letter, thinking it was from Francis. Who else would have written to her? But she knew instantly that couldn't have been so. The Emerald had come from the south and currently, the Lady Amelia was heading north their paths wouldn't have crossed. And anyway, why would Francis have written to her?

Then she recognised her mother's handwriting and seal. Mama had written!

She must have sent it shortly after the Lady Amelia left England for it to have arrived so speedily. Perhaps Mama had softened slightly towards her.

She opened the letter and read ...

'What's wrong?' Dinah said when she saw Georgiana's white face and trembling hands, 'Are you all right? Is it bad news?'

Georgiana nodded, silent tears coursing down her cheeks.

'My mother wrote to tell me she was dying. I expect she's dead by now,' she said, her voice lacking expression.

'I'm that sorry for you.'

'That isn't the bad news.'

'There's more?'

Georgiana nodded again, 'She wasn't my mother at all. I was adopted.'

Dinah put her arm around Georgiana's shoulders, 'That's a lot of bad news in one letter.'

'And do you know what the worst part of it is?' Georgiana said.

'There's more?'

'The worst part is that this letter arrived several days too late to change my life.'

Georgiana looked down at the letter in horror. She'd believed Fate couldn't touch her. When she'd learned Francis was her uncle, she thought she'd plumbed the depths of despair. But now she knew Francis wasn't a blood relation at all and their parting had been entirely unnecessary!

He'd sailed away from her and wouldn't discover what she knew for many months, perhaps years, if he didn't go home directly.

They could have been together, deserved to be together but now, it would never be. The depths of despair, it turned out, were far deeper than she could possibly ever have dreamed.

5

'Is she there?' Miss Chesterton asked, lightly touching Francis' arm. They were on deck, looking at the wharf which was lined with people waving goodbye to the Lady Amelia. Several women held babie's aloft for their sailor fathers to see for the last time and they waved until the men on the ship were too small to make out.

'I doubt it,' said Francis, 'Georgiana is working in the hospital. There's been another outbreak of smallpox. Surgeon White's very busy.'

'Even so,' said Miss Chesterton sliding her fingers across Francis' sleeve to gain a better hold of his arm, 'After all you meant to each other, surely she'd come and say goodbye.'

'We said our farewells,' Francis lied, forcing his voice to remain neutral. If he made it sound as though he were distraught — which indeed, he was — he suspected Miss Chesterton would take that as a challenge to do her Christian duty to comfort him. If he sounded as though he didn't care, she would take that as a signal he was available and willing. She was as subtle as a cannonball smashing through a window and she'd contrived enough accidental encounters for him to suspect she listened for the squeak as his cabin door opened and then followed him.

'If you'll excuse me; Miss Chesterton, I have much to do. I shall be especially busy on this leg of our journey.'

'Oh,' she said, biting her lower lip, 'And I had. thought with the convict women gone you and I might become better acquainted.'

'I'm afraid not, Miss Chesterton.'

He hurried away to the carpenter's shack further along the deck to get some grease for the hinges and lock to his cabin. '

'You'll be lucky,' grumbled the carpenter, 'That scoundrel Towler waited until we were ready to sail and then when me back was turned, stole some o' me tools and left. I knew 'e was planning to set up a carpenter's shop in Sydney butI didn't know it was going to be with the ship's tools. I've told Captain Yeats, but it's too late to go back now. I'll 'ave to make do. Ah, 'ere, use this,' he said finding a small, grimy tin. But I'll 'ave it back when you've finished, please sir. I can't afford to waste anything now.'

* * *

Reverend and Mrs Leston had disembarked in Sydney but the school teacher, Richard Everton, two .silk and porcelain merchants, and Mr and Miss Chesterton, had stayed aboard. Having faced gales, calms, extremes in temperature, food and water rationing as well as the putrid fever, bloody flux, gaol fever and scurvy, the remaining passengers had bonded into an unlikely group of companions who gathered most evenings in the captain's cabin for dinner.

Once Captain Yeats discovered that

Miss Chesterton had set her sights on his Naval· Agent, he ensured she was always seated next to Richard Everton, a square-chinned man with deep furrows on his brow who looked as if he was perpetually worried.

Captain Yeats knew that occasionally, Francis pretended that pressure· of work forced .him to avoid attending the dinners and he always corroborated his agent's story. The captain also knew that Francis was beginning to drink too much He'd lost focus ince the ship had sailed from Sydney and it was something to do with the convict woman — or more accurately, her absence.

From the beginning, Francis had been honest and told him he'd been appointed to his position on condition he looked out for the woman, a detail of which Captain Yeats had already been informed by the owner of the shipping company, Mr Russell. Whoever was so concerned about safeguarding the woman must be a man of influence if he had the ear of Mr Russell as well as being capable of arranging the appointment of Francis to the post of Agent of the Crown with special duties to protect one woman'.

At first, Captain Yeats had been resentful and ill-disposed towards the young lieutenant who he'd assumed had been foisted upon him with no idea of the job he was required to do. But Francis had shown a dedication and aptitude which far exceeded the captain's expectations. He'd also protected the woman in a quiet and dignified manner, and all had gone smoothly until Francis had fallen ill. After that, everything had changed and the captain had detected a spark in the relationship which hadn't been there before, despite the shows of feigned affection.

Captain Yeats had been dismayed at the prospect of losing such a fine Naval Agent at Sydney and he'd warned Francis. Love was all well and good but the conditions in Sydney, he knew, were exceedingly hard. Ship's masters returning from New South Wales had reported dwindling food supplies and failed crops.

In a settlement cqmprising mainly of convicts, the conditions would be difficult indeed and Captain Yeats wasn't convinced young love would survive.

Then mere hours later, Francis had changed his mind. A lovers' quarrel no doubt, but whatever the reason, the young man was now deeply troubled and as a result, he was drinking heavily.

Captain Yeats knew the signs: the slurred speech, the unsteady gait, the haggard face each morning. The captain, like most people, enjoyed a good brandy but he knew when to stop. That was something Francis had yet to learn and if he didn't want to find himself being forced into a marriage with that dreadful Quaker woman, he'd better learn quickly.

There was a knock at the door.

'Enter!' Captain Yeats called. He looked up as his clerk, Henry Talbot, entered, leading a tired looking, unshaven Francis into his cabin.

'Begging your pardon, captain …' Talbot said, which Captain Yeats took to mean, *I'm sorry we've been so long, captain*, knowing Talbot's usual punctuality.

The reason for the delay was obvious. Francis had overslept despite the bells marking each half hour of every watch. And Captain Yeats wasn't surprised. ·

'Sit down, lieutenant. Coffee?'

'Yes please.' Francis' voice was rasping as if his mouth were dry.

'Talbot, please fetch coffee.'

'Yes, captain.'

When the clerk had gone, Captain Yeats began to talk about the previous evening. He could tell from Francis' face that he remembered very little. And that was good because he wouldn't know when the captain embellished details slightly and he would be too embarrassed to ask any of the guests. He would simply have to believe what the captain said.

'You certainly charmed Miss Chesterton last night, lieutenant,' Captain Yeats said.

'Did I?' Francis groaned.

'Mr Everton was most vexed. And

214

as for Mr Chesterton ... But then you know how puritanical he is.'

Francis' bloodshot eyes opened wide, 'What happened?'

Talbot returned with the coffee and placed a cup in front of each man while the captain described what had taken place the previous evening.

'I take it from your reaction now that it was the brandy talking last night?' The captain asked.

Francis nodded, then winced at the motion of his head.

'So, are you actually interested in the Quaker woman or not?'

''No!'

'God's blood, man! Then sort yourself out!'

When Francis had gone, Talbot remarked, 'The lieutenant hasn't been himself since his convict woman left. Is he really after that dreadful Miss Chesterton?'

'No, Lieutenant Brooks isn't interested in her at all. He's simply drinking to try to forget the convict woman.'

'It sounds like he's stirring up a hornets' nest if he behaves like that, captain.'

'Well,' Captain Yeat.s said, leaning back in his chair and placing his pipe in his mouth, 'I may have exaggerated his behaviour last night slightly, but since Lieutenant Brooks didn't query my words, I assume he didn't notice my elaboration and that means that he was too drunk to know or to remember what he was doing or saying. If he believes he acted more rashly than he did, hopefully, he'll be at pains to remedy the situation in future. You might call it strategic falsehood.'

'Ah!', said Talbot as a slow smile crept across his gnarled face, 'For the young fellow's own good, eh, captain?'

★ ★ ★

Francis apologised to Mr Chesterton for behaving inappropriately towards his daughter, blaming his foolishness on too much brandy. Mr Chesterton appeared slightly puzzled, but nevertheless; he accepted the apology although couldn't resist a small lecture and pressed home his point with a verse from the Bible.

'Remember the Book of Ephesians, chapter five and verse eighteen,' he said gravely, 'And be not drunk with wine, wherein is excess, but be filled with the Spirit.'

He seemed to be warming to his theme, so Francis assured him he'd learned his lesson.

'So, you're saying, Lieutenant, you were pleasant to me because you'd drunk too much brandy?' Miss Chesterton looked as though she were about to cry and Francis didn't trust himself to speak without hurting her feelings further. He excused himself and hurried away, determined to keep out of their way.

How could he have been so foolish? He certainly didn't remember doing and saying all the things Captain Yeats had claimed but then he didn't remember much at all.

It wouldn't happen again. But how many other times had he told himself that?

He seemed to go up hill and down dale on his journey through life. Firstly, he'd rushed headlong downhill, overindulging in women, gambling and liquor, then when he realised how self-destructive his life had become, he'd grabbed the opportunity Thomas had given him to regain his self-respect and had climbed to the top of the hill.

He'd fallen for Georgiana and planned a normal, worthwhile life with her, only to discover their love was forbidden. Now, he wanted to drink to forget and once again, he was sliding into the valley. And once again, he knew that when he reached the bottom, he'd lose the ability to care, much less have the wherewithal to start climbing to the top.

What would be the point? There was nothing on the peak. Not for him, anyway. He'd wanted to be with Georgiana. No one else would do. He decided he'd go back to England. He wanted to confront Thomas, the man who he'd thought so honourable. And then, he'd take the money his brother-in-law had promised him and... well, he'd make his mind up then. Or perhaps he'd drink himself into a stupor until the money ran out.

★ ★ ★

Captain Yeats lit his pipe, leaned back in his chair and, placing his hands on his ample paunch, he surveyed Francis on the other side of the table.

'Have you given any thought to what you'll do when we reach Canton?'

Francis looked up from his book and laid his quill down, 'Was there something in particular you wanted done?'

'I don't mean ship's business. I mean where you'll go from there.'

'If you're referring to Miss Chesterton's invitation to stay with her in Canton, I'll definitely not be taking that up!'

'Poor Mr Everton. He's smitten· with the woman. Can't abide her, myself. Still, there's no accounting for taste, is there? Well, if you're not in Canton, distracting her, she might turn her attentions to him.'

'If I'm not in Canton?' Francis asked with a puzzled frown, 'I'll be there as long as the Lady Amelia is there.' ·

'Well ...' The captain drew on his pipe and blew out a cloud of smoke, 'I was wondering if it wouldn't be a good idea for you to seek passage on a ship bound for New South Wales.'

He held his hand up to stop Francis' protest,

'You haven't been the same since you left that girl of yours. There's no point denying it. As ship's master, I've spent much of my life cheek by jowl with all manner of men. They might not say much but I'm good at reading their silences ... And I know you're hurting.'

'I've cut down on my drinking and I'm trying'

'I don't doubt it, Francis. And it's not your work I'm criticising. I have a wife and two daughters in Kent. The last time .I saw them, the girls were as tall as my shoulder. The next time I see them, it's possible I might walk past them in the street and not know them. They barely know me. I see my wife rarely and I know she can't wait until I've gone to sea again. I disrupt their lives. I send money but other than that, I have no significance in their world. Whose fault is that?' He drew on his pipe again and as he exhaled, he watched the smoke rise to the cabin ceiling, 'My fault, of course. I chose the sea. It's where I feel most alive. But you, Francis, you're a good sailor and a good agent but this isn't where you belong. Go back to Sydney. Find the woman and tell her. What's holding you back, man?'

Francis stared down at his. book, ''There are things that would prevent... that is... ' He shook his head and sighed, 'It just can't be.'

'Look, I don't know what the problem is but everything can be sorted out! You don't need to confide in me but I'm guessing it's something to — do with previous commitments and I know you're an honourable man but in Sydney, it's as if the rule book's been torn up. The whole settlement is a huge experiment and for it to work, men and women have to settle down and work hard. They have to raise families like they would've back in England. Of course, many of them already have wives and husbands at home but what's the point of remaining faithful to someone you'll never see again? You can't keep men and women apart so the authorities bow to the inevitable and although it's not official policy, everyone turns a blind eye, even encourages it — including the priest who carries out the weddings. Everyone pretends previous commitments don't exist. So why don't you? Whatever impediment is preventing you from being with that woman can be overcome.' He patted Francis on the shoulder, 'Think it over.'

His words, although kindly meant, felt as though they'd pierced Francis' heart. The impediment preventing him being with Georgiana could not be put aside. It was final. It was insurmountable. It was blood. And for Francis to pretend otherwise was unpardonable.

It was many months before the Lady Amelia docked in London. Francis had decided against his plan to confront Thomas. After all, there probably wasn't a father in the land who wouldn't protect his daughter and if that meant sacrificing someone else, so be it. Thomas had merely taken care of his little girl and the price had been Georgiana — the daughter of his sister-in-law — merely a niece by marriage.

And to Thomas' credit, he'd taken steps to look after his niece which was probably more than many would have done. In fact, he'd taken a chance in pleading . for her sentence to be reduced to transportation. If she'd been hanged, no one would have found out about Margaret's unfortunate weakness.

It wasn't Thomas' fault that Francis had fallen in love with his own niece.

So, there was no need to go to Meadmayne House to see Thomas or the sisters he barely knew. He'd simply write to let them know he'd returned safely. He hoped Thomas would fulfil his side of the bargain and pay the sum he'd promised but now, his brother-in-law's money seemed tarnished, so if he'd changed his mind, Francis wouldn't have been upset. After all, he didn't plan to buy a house and settle down. He'd join Captain Yeats again aboard the lady Amelia after it had been repaired, and they'd sail to Jamaica for a cargo of sugar. Perhaps the captain had been wrong, perhaps Francis did belong at sea. There was certainly nowhere else he felt at home or at peace.

He took lodgings in a dilapidated house in Deptford, poring over the newspapers for articles about the new colony in Sydney and waiting to set sail. When he'd written to Thomas and Alice, he'd given the address 9f the shipping company who owned the lady Amelia but no reply had come and he'd accepted Thomas had no intention of paying him the sum he'd promised.

Well, he'd cleared Francis' debts before he'd sailed to Sydney. That was sufficient. Other than the shabby rooms he was renting and his food, he had no other expenses and soon, he'd be sailing away on the lady Amelia, .

When there was a knock at his door, he assumed it was Mrs Proudfoot, the landlady, come for the rent, so he was astonished to see Alice and Thomas standing there with Mrs Proudfoot hovering in the background.

'Everything all right, sir?' she asked, obviously interested in her lodger's rich visitors.

'Yes, thank you, Mrs Proudfoot,' Francis said, ushering Alice and Thomas in to his room.

'Shall I bring tea, sir?'

'No thank you,' Alice said holding a handkerchief to her nose, 'My husband and I will not be staying long.'

'As you wish, ma'am,' Mrs Proudfoot said, still lingering on the stairs.

'If I'd known you were staying in squalor, I'd have insisted you come to stay with us at Meadmayne House,' Thomas said glancing around the dingy room with its worn-out furnishings.

'I'll help you pack up now,' Alice said, 'The coach leaves in an hour and you must come back and stay with us.'

'That's very kind but I sail in a few days,' Francis said, trying to hide his annoyance at his sister's overbearing manner, 'I'll stay here.'

'Nonsense,' said Alice, 'Your letter was delayed or we'd have been here before. But now we've come all this way to find you and I have to say, Francis, you didn't make it very easy. Although I can see why you wouldn't have wanted to give this address.' She sat down and pulled her skirts onto her lap, away from the dusty chair. 'But having visited the shipping company's offices and then had to come here,' she wrinkled her nose, 'You owe it to us to come back to Meadmayne House. Thomas asked Mr Russell if he could spare you for a few days and he said he could, didn't he Thomas?'

Francis was about to tell her he trad no intention of travelling with them to Essex when Alice cut in, 'Before you consider refusing our invitation, I have to tell you we have an ulterior motive in taking you home with us ... It's been a very trying time for our family and I'm afraid we have some sad news for you, Francis,' She paused fora few seconds, 'I'm afraid our dear sister, Cecile, tragically died many weeks ago while you were at sea. Now you've returned, we propose to hold a memorial service. So, you see, you must return with us.'

Francis felt the colour drain from his face, not because he was grief-stricken at the death of a sister he'd hardly known, but because he couldn't imagine what Georgiana was doing now on the other side of the world, completely oblivious to the death of her mother.

'I realise you didn't have much of an opportunity to get to know Cecile when you were growing up but she obviously had feelings for you because you and I are both equal beneficiaries in her will.'

'With her daughter?' Francis asked. 'Gracious, no!' Alice said, 'Just you and me. To be honest, I'm rather shocked at how much she had in savings. Thomas and I were under the misapprehension she was completely impoverished, and yet she had quite a tidy sum.'

'But surely she's made provision for her own daughter?' Francis realised he'd raised his voice and was almost shouting.

Alice shrank back in surprise, 'If Georgiana had been her daughter, I expect Cecile would have left something to her.'

Francis stared at his sister for several seconds, then finally managed, 'If Georgiana had been her daughter? What do you mean if?'

Thomas leaned forward and placed a hand on Francis' arm as if to reassure him. 'Now, Francis, I don't want you to be concerned. We all believed she was Cecile's daughter and I asked you in good faith to look after her. I understand from Captain Yeats you did a fine job and simply because it transpires she's not our flesh and blood at all, you will be paid in full. Trust me on that.'

'Not our flesh and blood?' Francis said, pressing his palms to his temples.

'Francis! I had no idea you'd be affected by this. After all, you haven't had much contact with Cecile for many years. If I'd known you were going to be so upset, I'd have prepared you first,' Alice said, 'But in all truth, it came as a great shock to Thomas and myself. The first we knew about the scandal was the morning Cecile died. She'd been writing this ...' Alice fished in her bag and held out a letter towards Francis.

'The entire story is in there. Writing this was the last thing Cecile did before she died. It was as though she remained alive long enough to ensure we knew the truth about the imposter. Who'd have thought Joshua could be so heartless as to pass off his mistress' daughter as an orphan? I knew he was feckless but I'd never have suspected that of him!'

Francis read the letter, then reread it to make sure he'd understood every word. He silently handed it back to Alice.

'There's no doubt it tells the truth,' Alice said, tucking the letter back in her bag, 'I can't believe she didn't tell me before. Thomas and I took her in when she was in desperate need and I'd have thought she'd have confided in her only sister. Imagine! Keeping that secret to yourself for years!'

But Francis wasn't listening. He abruptly stood up and strode to the door.

'Francis? Francis! Where are you going?' Alice called after him as he ran down the stairs two at a time and hurried out onto the busy street.

He had to get away from Alice's inane chatter and Thomas' largesse and assurances that he would be paid in full. What did he care if his elder sister had kept a secret for years? Or that he'd be paid a penny?

He'd found the perfect woman and circumstances had decreed that he must leave her on the other side of the world, abandon all hopes of ever seeing her again and put all thoughts of her from his mind. And now he'd discovered that the circumstances had been the result of lies and deceit!

Georgiana and he could have made a

life together. They could have been married by now and settled in Sydney but instead, they were as far apart as it was possible to be.

Francis hurried along through the streets. He'd go to see Captain Yeats and explain why he couldn't join the Lady Amelia on its voyage to Jamaica and ask for his help in getting passage as quickly as possible to New South Wales.

6

'Have you finished the *Smilax glyci-phylla*, Duchess?' David Oakley asked as he entered his office.

'Almost,' Georgiana said, looking up from the paper where she'd been sketching the leaves.

'Good. Here's the description for you to copy.' He stood behind her and inspected the picture, 'That's excellent. How lucky I am to have you.'

As he studied her sketch, his breath brushed her neck and she began to feel uncomfortable at his closeness. Nevertheless, although he placed a hand on the back of the chair, he didn't touch her or give her any reason to move away and she recognised he might simply be engrossed in the drawing, inspecting it in the minutest detail. It would be presumptuous to assume otherwise.

Assistant-Surgeon David Oakley had a special interest in native remedies and he'd been pleased to assist John White in compiling information which they hoped to publish. However, David's earlier sketches of plants had not been very realistic. He was meticulous in his records, noting all the beneficial properties of each part of a plant and arguably, he was as good at identifying the different species as John White, but his drawings were usually smudged and out of proportion.

Shortly after Dinah's midshipman had sailed away, she'd lost his baby and it had taken her some time to recover. But since she and Georgiana had both studied Surgeon Dawes' illustrations of tropical flora while aboard the Lady Amelia, they had more idea than the other nurses about herbs and plants, and Surgeon White arranged for an armed marine to accompany them in the forest to protect them from natives while they collected specimens.

Peaceful walks had helped Dinah recuperate and both women enjoyed their expeditions to gather plants. On one occasion, Georgiana spotted a herb which resembled the native spinach and having been unable to reach it, she'd studied it, then on returning to the hospital, she'd drawn it from memory. Surgeon White had been impressed with her powers of recall and her artistic skills and David had asked her to help him with his work.

Despite her lowly position as a convict, he'd always treated her with respect. However, recently, she'd looked up unexpectedly to find him studying her. He often lingered nearby and sometimes even placed a hand lightly on her arm but if he had feelings for her, he never expressed them. Not surprising, Georgiana told herself, as it was unlikely a man of his standing would be interested in a convict.

But Dinah said she'd noticed a change in his behaviour and she urged Georgiana not to be so aloof. 'Surgeon Oakley's taken a fancy to you, Duchess. You'd be a fool not to encourage him. He's good looking, kind and Surgeon

White favours him above his other assistants. What's the matter with you?'

Mary, who'd started Georgiana's nickname of Duchess, had made similar comments about David, and coaxed Georgiana to encourage him. Yet something held Georgiana back. Something or someone who she'd vowed never to bring to mind again.

During the months she'd been in Sydney, she'd managed to suppress her emotions. If she didn't allow herself to feel anything, then nothing could hurt her. And with such emptiness inside, it would be hard to care for a man again.

There was a knock at the door and without waiting to be invited in, Rose, one of the nurses entered. 'Hope I'm not disturbing anything,' she said with a smirk as David stepped back abruptly.

'Of course not!' he said, his voice tinged with irritation.

Rose was the hospital gossip and from her knowing smile, she obviously thought she'd discovered something new.

'Only, I was looking for the Duchess. Surgeon Harrison's askin' fer her. There's a couple o' them natives come in with a young'un covered in small-pox spots. The surgeon's having such a job makin' em understand! Anyway, he needs the Duchess to help.' She turned to go, 'Bloomin' natives!' she said under her breath.

Georgiana rose to follow.

'You have such a good heart,' David said to her as she left.

Surgeon Harrison was speaking slowly and loudly but to no avail. The native woman's eyes were wide with fear and as the doctor began to shout, she backed away, holding the limp child closer to her.

'I cannot do anything to help you unless you let me look at the child!' the doctor shouted.

The native man stepped between the doctor and his woman.

'Oh, Duchess!' Surgeon Harrison said, his face registering relief, 'Please can you let these savages know I'm not going to hurt the child ...'

Georgiana stepped forward and smiled at the family, greeting them in the language of the Eora people which she'd picked up from other patients and an Eora girl who'd recovered from small-pox and had stayed for a while to help in the hospital.

On hearing Georgiana's gentle voice speaking their language, the woman's lower lip began to quiver but her eyes filled with hope and the man relaxed his hostile stance. The mother spoke slowly and clearly. Nevertheless, Georgiana only understood a few words, but it was enough to know the parents had walked for several days to reach the hospital which they'd been told was the only way of saving their son.

She relayed what she'd learned to Surgeon Harrison and using signs and a few words, finally, the child was put in a cot.

'The parents'll get it next,' the surgeon said, rolling his eyes, 'I expect they'll take themselves off into the bush and spread it around even further making more work for us. I cannot conceive how they summon the courage to come here for treatment. If it wasn't for the natives and their unprovoked attacks against our people we wouldn't have half as many patients. I've never seen so many spear wounds! Yet they consider it acceptable to come here with smallpox.'

'But they don't know how to treat smallpox,' Georgiana said, 'None of their people had it before we came, so I think it's the least we can do to help them!'

Surgeon Harrison snorted.

Georgiana knew his opinions were shared by many of the settlers. It was true the natives stole food from their crops and their fishing catches and in a settlement where food supplies were inadequate, that was obviously a cause of friction.

But the natives hadn't asked the British to settle on their land. Georgiana wondered if perhaps they saw the fish and plants as belonging to them. If so, no one should be surprised if they took what they considered theirs already.

As for unprovoked attacks, that wasn't

true. It was often later shown that men who'd been wounded by natives in what they claimed were unprovoked attacks, had actually been stealing souvenirs such as throwing sticks, spears and fishing nets. There'd been faults on both sides but since the natives had not invited anyone to settle on their land, Georgiana's sympathy lay with them.

She'd looked into the eyes of the frightened native women who'd walked great distances to bring their lesion smothered children to the hospital and had seen the same feelings as she saw in the eyes of settler women who came to see the doctor with a sick child. She recognised identical emotions in all women: love, desperation, fear and hope. The skin colour, language and customs of the natives might be different but to treat them as little better than animals, was cruel and inhuman.

Against all odds, the young boy survived and shortly after, the parents took their son and disappeared from whence they came.

★ ★ ★

One day, Georgiana realised that in three weeks' time, the convicts who'd arrived on the Lady Amelia would have been in Sydney for one whole year ...

It'd been a difficult time with crop failures leading to food shortages which in turn had driven desperate people to steal from their neighbours. The courts had been busy and several people were hanged from the large fig tree on the eastern side of the cove. But there were now signs that the farms which had been established in Parramatta might be making some headway with food production and several ships had brought additional supplies and letters from England.

The arrival of such vessels was always a cause for celebration for the population of Sydney who gathered on the wharf to watch the longboats row ashore. All except Georgiana who couldn't bear to see ships arrive, much less leave. It was harder to keep the memories suppressed with such reminders anchored in the cove.

As she and Dinah set out to the woods to gather plants with their marine guard, many people were hurrying excitedly to see the provisions being brought ashore. Usually, Dinah would have wanted to watch the spectacle but Georgiana knew she'd be happy to go to the woods because she and the marine sergeant who'd been assigned to escort them on their expeditions had fallen in love, and they took every opportunity to steal away. It meant that Georgiana was left to gather herbs, berries and leaves alone and if anyone noticed the two women didn't bring much back, they must have assumed that the particular leaves they'd been seeking had been hard to find.

Ralph Simpson, the sergeant who'd been detailed to accompany the two women to the forest, met them at the hospital and led them away from the crowds who were heading in the opposite direction towards the shore.

A man slipped out of the carpenter's shop and made his way against the tide of people, following the trio, keeping a constant distance behind them. It wasn't the first time he'd tailed the two women and their guard and he knew that once they were hidden from view, the sergeant would take the hand of the small, blonde woman and they'd slip away, leaving the dark-haired woman alone in the forest.

Today, was the day the one they called the Duchess would pay for past insults.

★ ★ ★

It was lucky there was a plentiful supply of *Smilax glyciphylla*, or sweet sarsaparilla, Georgiana thought, because so far, David's attempts to cultivate it had been unsuccessful. It was a useful plant which in the absence of plentiful fruit and vegetables, could be brewed into a tea that prevented scurvy. Georgiana chewed a leaf slowly, releasing the sweet flavour. She wished Ralph and Dinah would return. The vegetation was dense in this part of the forest with rustling and scuffling in the undergrowth which suggested she was surrounded by numerous unseen animals, possibly, she thought, with a shiver of fear, snakes.

A scraping sound from above attracted her attention and she looked up into a tall tree to see a small, furry face with a pointed nose peeping at her. The possum seemed to be as fascinated with her as she was with it and she stepped backwards slowly, keeping her eyes on the animal so she could see its body.

The stench of bad breath hit her first and before she could turn, a hand clamped over her mouth, dragging her backwards so sharply, she overbalanced. Her first thought was that Dinah was playing a stupid trick but the calloused hand was gripping her too tightly and pulling her too roughly.

She realised it was a man's breath, heavy and ragged in her ear.

'Duchess,' he whispered.

Now she knew exactly who it was.

Arthur Towler.

With one hand on her mouth, he wrapped the other around her body, pinning her arms to her side, as he dragged her backwards, her feet scrabbled vainly at the ground trying to find her footing. His strong, workmen's hands felt as though they were crushing her skull and she tried to claw them from her mouth and nose so she could breathe. Suddenly he grunted and stopped. There was a thud and a jolt as if he'd backed into a tree, then he screamed.

As he let her go, she fell backwards, her legs tangled in her petticoats and it was a second before she realised what had happened.

Silently, a native had crept up behind Towler and had thrust a spear into his shoulder. Georgiana got to her knees, her boots still tangled in her skirts, expecting to feel a blow on her back but the native wasn't looking at her.

'Werre! Werre!' he said insistently to the prostrate figure of Towler, his lip curled in contempt. Georgiana had heard natives use the word before when shouting at the settlers. It meant 'Go away!'

The native helped Georgiana to her feet and nodding once, as if in salute, he strode away and slipped into the shadows.

* * *

The rumours were rife. The truth that one of their own had attacked a nurse in the woods and a native had saved her, was so unbelievable that most people had made up their own story. After all, the Duchess hadn't been alone. She'd been with another nurse and a guard. No, it must have been yet another unprovoked attack by a native on one of the settlers. Although no one could explain Towler's part in the incident. Possibly he'd been out for a stroll and had inadvertently been caught up in the attack.

The spearhead was removed from Towler's shoulder and when he'd recovered, he was tried and found guilty of assault although many rallied to his side and the governor decided to send him away to the penal colony on Norfolk Island. Once in the middle of the Pacific Ocean, he'd soon be forgotten and relations between the settlers and natives would hopefully be restored.

Dinah and Ralph Simpson were both punished when it was revealed they'd, left Georgiana on her own. Again, many believed there was a conspiracy to implicate settlers and absolve natives.

David Oakley was one of the few who believed Georgiana's story. Towler had remained silent regarding his intentions towards Georgiana. He'd been carrying a knife at the time of the attack but as he'd pointed out, he was a free man and therefore at liberty to carry one. No one would know what he'd planned, although it was obvious he'd been intent on mischief and with that thought uppermost in his mind, the usually shy David Oakley was driven to proclaim his love to Georgiana and to propose, so that he could take care of her in the future.

'What d'you mean you didn't say yes?'

Dinah asked, her voice rising in disbelief when Georgiana told her, 'Pish, Duchess! Sometimes I wonder at your sanity!'

'Pish yerself!' Mary said, 'Just because you'd throw yerself at the first man who looks your way!'

'That's not true! Ralph and me's gain' to get wed as soon as we can. He's the man for me!'

Mary raised her eyebrows and sniffed, 'Until he looks elsewhere an' then yer'll have a new man in the blink of an eye!'

Dinah turned her back on Mary, 'So, why did you turn 'im down? He's kind an' he obviously adores you!' …

'I didn't actually turn him down, I just said I'd have to think about it.'

Dinah groaned, 'You have to get them to the parson as soon as yer can before they change their mind.'

'And have yer thought about it an' decided, Duchess?' Mary asked.

'Yes, I'll marry him but not until I'm free,' Georgiana said.

Dinah pointed out, 'But if yer take into account the time you were in prison in England, the voyage here an' the year just gone, you've still got more than four years to serve. You're expecting him to wait that long?'

'If 'e loves her, 'e'll wait an' if not, 'e's not worth havin',' Mary said.

'The trouble is,' Georgiana said, 'I'm not sure I'll ever love him and that wouldn't be fair.'

'Yer don't want to worry about details like that, Duchess,' Dinah said, 'Surgeon Oakley'll look after you. And that's all that matters.'

'When will you tell him?' Mary asked.

'Later. David. and Surgeon White have gone along the coast to look for Goat's Foot. When he gets back, I'll tell him...'

'Well, let's hope he doesn't change his mind,' Dinah said shaking her head in disbelief.

'As if that's likely to 'appen,' said Mary, 'you can see 'e worships the ground she walks on. 'E'll wait till the end of time if that's what it takes.'

★ ★ ★

There was to be no wedding. At the same time as Georgiana was telling Dinah and Mary about the proposal, David and Surgeon White were walking along the coast looking for the creeping, evergreen, plants that were known as Goat's Foot which often grew on the upper region of beaches. Two fishermen had been stung by stingrays and were in hospital in great pain. The native cure was Goat's Foot leaf sap and Surgeon White wanted to gather some to test.

The doctors found a cove covered in the dense growth and while Surgeon White made a few sketches, David picked leaves and dug into the soil to pull up roots. It would be more convenient, if he could grow the plants closer to the hospital but as he delved among the vegetation, he dislodged a rock, beneath which a snake was hidden. It bit him before slithering away into the Goat's Foot tangle.

Surgeon White half-carried David back to the hospital but he died shortly after.

★ ★ ★

David had deserved better, Georgiana thought. He was young, intelligent, kind and thoughtful. He'd deserved a longer life to fulfil his promise and he'd deserved the love of a woman who'd wanted to marry him above all else. If she'd truly loved him, it wouldn't have mattered whether she was free or not. But then, she'd always been honest that she didn't love him.

Perhaps one day, with David's patience and goodness, he might have worn away the outer shell she'd constructed to separate her from all emotion and she would have allowed his love to touch her. But that would never happen now.

If ever there was a lesson to learn from this latest tragedy to blight her life, it was to remain strong and resolute.

Love had no place in her world now.

7

The look-out on the southern head signalled the arrival of the long awaited supply ship, Peregrine, to the authorities in Sydney and as the message spread around town, people gathered on the shore and wharf to watch and celebrate. It had been some time since a ship had arrived with supplies and it was widely whispered that London had forgotten about the convict settlement which would be left to either become self-sufficient or to starve.

If the settlers were pleased to see the Peregrine, the crew were no less pleased to see Sydney. The winds had been against them most of the way and a collision with another vessel in Table Bay had resulted in unscheduled time in Cape Town. The unfavourable winds had ensured the final leg of the journey took longer than expected and with dwindling supplies, many of the sailors became scorbutic. But now at last the Peregrine had reached harbour.

Weak from fever and suffering the early symptoms of scurvy, Francis was first out of the longboat. He waited impatiently on the wharf for his baggage to be unloaded, then having engaged a man with a handcart to convey it to a nearby inn, he plunged into the crowd, checking every female face for Georgiana's.

At the inn, Francis paid a week in advance for a room and left the innkeeper to arrange to have his chest and bags taken up, then he immediately left. He knew it was most unlikely he'd encounter Georgiana in the street, nevertheless, he scanned every woman's face as he walked briskly towards Governor Phillip's residence where the records of all the convicts would be kept. It was possible she'd still be working in the hospital but he knew from the London newspapers that many convicts were now working several miles from Sydney, in Parramatta, while others were settling along the banks of the Hawkesbury River. The governor would know exactly where she was.

The servant who opened the door said Governor Phillips and his clerk had gone to Parramatta for a few days or possibly more and said she was sorry she couldn't help him because she wasn't allowed to touch anything in the governor's office. He asked for directions for the hospital and set off across the Tank Stream, to the western side of Sydney.

'Can I help you, sir?' a nurse asked as Francis approached the long hospital building.

'I'm looking for Georgiana Aylwood. I believe she works here.'

The nurse tilted her head to one side as she considered the name, 'No, sir, I'm sorry, I don't believe there's anyone by that name working here, but I haven't been here long. If you wait, I'll ask someone.'

The nurse appeared at the door a few moments later with a puzzled frown, 'I'm sorry, sir, but she says she's never heard of 'er. An' if Mary don't know 'er, she don't war 'ere.'

'Has 'e gone?' Mary was waiting inside the hospital, behind the door and she caught Rose's wrist as she passed.

'Ow! What you doin' that for?' She pulled her arm away from Mary, 'Yes 'e's gone. 'E looked really sad.'

'And well 'e might look sad!' Mary said, her lip curled in contempt.

'I thought 'e seemed really nice. How do you know 'im?'

'Never you mind.'

'So, who is Georgiana Aylwood.'

'It ain't nothin' to do with you.'

'All right. I was just askin',' Rose said. She hurried away, rubbing her wrist.

Mary had been passing the door with a pile of clean linen when she'd seen Rose stop and talk to a man and she'd carried on walking a few steps before she realised who he was. She'd hidden out of sight listening and wondering what Lieutenant Brooks was doing back in Sydney asking for Georgiana.

Duchess, Mary's nickname for Geor-

254

giana, had become so popular, very few now remembered her real name. It suited her so well. Dignified and intelligent, Georgiana obviously didn't belong among the convict women. She'd never spoken about her crime and Mary suspected she'd been wrongfully sentenced. It wouldn't be the first time the courts had been unjust. Georgiana never pleaded innocence like so many, when it was obvious they were guiltier than Lucifer. Mary knew nothing about Georgiana's past other than that she'd spent the entire voyage as Lieutenant Brooks' sea-wife and then on arrival in Sydney, he'd discarded her and sailed off.

Mary had been jealous of the preferential treatment Georgiana had received aboard ship and at every opportunity, she'd made her life miserable. She'd known her poisoned barbs hit home but Georgiana had refused to respond. It was obviously her way of dealing with pain. Whereas Mary lashed out, encouraging the fierce reputation she'd earned in an effort to prevent further hurt, Georgiana had simply denied her feelings. And yet, she still had love to give to others, that was obvious from the way she treated each patient, even the natives. And it had been Georgiana who'd recommended Mary for the job in the hospital. Few people had cared enough about Mary to do her a good turn.

There was something special about the Duchess and although Mary would never admit it to anyone, she intended to look out for her. So, it was best that Lieutenant Brooks left on the Peregrine without Georgiana ever knowing.

'Mary? Are you well? You look troubled.' It was Georgiana, peering at her in alarm.

'Me? Yes, fine!' Mary said quickly.

'Betsy asked me to tell you the water you wanted has boiled ...' Georgiana said.

'About time!' Mary said, hurrying away with the linen, keen for Georgiana to move away from the door in case Lieutenant Brooks returned.

Suppose he came back to the hospital? He might ask someone who would remember the Duchess' real name. Or suppose he met her by chance in the street? Mary decided she would put an end to Lieutenant Brooks' search and save Georgiana further hurt.

★   ★   ★

It had been easy to find the lieutenant. For the price of a drink, one of the Peregrine's sailors told her where he was staying. Francis was eating dinner alone when she entered the inn.

'Lieutenant Brooks?'

He looked up with a guarded expression, obviously expecting her to offer him her services.

'I understand you was lookin' fer Georgiana.'

'Yes!' He dropped his knife and stood, holding out the chair for her to sit at his table.

'Is this woman troublin' yer, sir?' the innkeeper asked scowling at Mary.

'No, she's a guest, thank you.'

'Whatever yer say, sir.' He glared at Mary.

'Do you know where she is?' Francis asked.

'She died a few months back,' Mary said.

The colour drained from his face and he looked as though she'd punched him in the stomach. He was fighting back tears and it took several moments before he was able to ask, 'How?'

'Putrid fever.'

He pushed the half-eaten dinner away, staring into the distance trying to take the terrible information in. 'Where's she buried?'

'Buried?' Mary hadn't thought that far ahead, 'Oh, buried. Yes, well... that would be in a paupers' grave in the cemetery.'

'Will you show me where?'

'I don't know where. It's unmarked.'

'You mean no headstone?'

'No. We're convicts. No one cares if we've got headstones.'

'Well, I do. I'll have one made for her.'

'No! You can't!' Mary said, her voice rising in panic, 'She's not here. She was taken away.'

'But you said she was in the cemetery ...'

'And so she is... but not here.'

'Then where?'

'I don't know!' Mary cried rising so fast, the chair toppled, 'She's gone! Best you go home!' She hurried to the door without looking back.

* * *

She died a few months back. At the woman's words, the world had stopped. Colour had drained away as if everything had turned to stone. For months, he'd dreamed of finding Georgiana and telling her the good news that they weren't related and that they were free to love. It had kept him going during the long voyage.

And now? No, it couldn't be true.

The woman had been most insistent. But who was she? He realised he hadn't even asked her name. As soon as she'd mentioned Georgiana, he'd wanted to know where she was and then once the woman had uttered those words, his mind had gone numb.

The red-headed woman obviously knew more than she was saying. If only he'd asked who she was and where he could contact her. She wasn't well-known in the inn, or the innkeeper would have recognised her. Francis rose. If he hurried, he might find her although he'd allowed precious moments to slip away while he replayed the conversation in his mind.

Stepping out into the street, he tried to recall her appearance. She was tall with red hair and sharp fea-tures ... he suddenly recalled where he'd seen her before. She'd been the troublemaker on the Lady Amelia. He remembered her well. She'd been in irons several times for fighting... and she'd taken a special dislike to Georgiana.

Francis began to run along the street.

Ahead, in a crowd of people, he thought he could see the woman. Mary, that was her name, Mary Norris.

★ ★ ★

Although darkness had fallen, he could see the figure hurrying ahead along the street had red hair but he wasn't convinced he was following the right woman. If he wasn't, then he would never find Mary again. Even if it was her, at any moment, she might turn off and disappear in the darkness.

'Mary!' he called and as she stopped and turned, searching the faces of the bystanders for someone she knew, she recognised Francis and with a gasp of surprise, she began to run, turning into a narrow side street. He caught her easily.

'I know who you are,' he said, gasping for breath, 'I remember you from the ship.'

'So?' She was defiant

'I want to know where Georgiana is

and why you told me she'd died.' He sent up a fervent prayer that Mary had been lying and when she didn't repeat the claim, he knew he'd been right.

Mary merely glared at him insolently, with hands on hips. 'I don't 'ave to tell you nothin',' she said and turned as if to walk away.

As he reached out to grab her arm to stop her, he suddenly became aware of the whisper of air past his ear, then a tremendous pain on the side of his head.

Then blackness.

8

Georgiana walked the length of the hospital, her lantern held high as she checked each patient. How many times had she done this before? Her late-night checks were now routine, but tonight, they held a special significance.

Not that anyone would have known by looking at her; there were no visible signs unless they noticed she was walking taller, her head held higher. The previous night as she'd carried out her rounds, she'd caught sight of her shadow on the wall. It walked in time with her, stopping at each bed when she stopped. It was familiar and comforting and the sudden confirmation had come that she belonged here, in Sydney, in this hospital. This was her home.

Once, she'd planned to go back to England but now there was nothing to return for. No family she wanted to see and by now, Francis would be married and settled down, or if not, he'd be sailing the high seas.

She still dreamed of him. However much she managed to suppress her memories there was no way to control her dreams, and always, it was the same dream. He'd sail into Sydney and she'd see him on deck but although she rowed towards him as hard as she could, the ship's sails filled with wind and the gap between them widened until he was merely a dot on the horizon.

When she'd believed they were close relatives, shame had forced Francis from her mind. When she'd learned the truth, and realised they had every right to be together, Francis was on the Lady Amelia sailing north, further and further out of her life and it had been too painful to have him in her thoughts. Now, she had no idea where he was nor any prospect of finding him, so it was best he remained locked away in the darkest recesses of her memory if she was to find peace.

One thing was certain, England was no longer home. Sydney was where she belonged. This new colony which was constantly adapting to the adverse conditions. The heat, insects, poor soils and countless other problems were tackled with ingenuity using the settlement's meagre resources and unusual population. Convicts had been enlisted to run farms and catch fish. Recently they formed, first the Night Watch, then the Sydney Foot Police to protect people from those who never abandoned their criminal habits.

There were many opportunities in Sydney which wouldn't have been available in England and Georgiana planned to take full advantage. That morning, she'd asked Surgeon White if she could assume more duties. Nervously, she'd told him she wanted to be a surgeon and had braced herself for his derision and a firm rejection. But he'd listened patiently while she justified her request, pointing out she'd observed many operations and knew a great deal about herbs and other remedies while acknowledging she had much to learn but if they'd give her a chance ...

Remembering that moment when he'd smiled and said she'd make an excellent surgeon, she was filled with a rush of optimism for the first time since... well, the first time ever.

* * *

Members of the Sydney Foot Police were regular visitors to the hospital, bringing victims of violence or drunkards who'd been injured during brawls. As Georgiana reached the end of the rows of beds, she heard voices approaching and as she looked out, she saw members of the Foot Police carrying two men and helping a woman towards her.

'Mary?' Georgiana gasped when she recognised the woman and saw she was limping and bracing her arm as if it was broken.

Surgeon Harrison was on duty. He listened to the details and he called Rose and Dinah to help with the new patients, leaving Georgiana to take care of Mary.

'Mary! What happened?' Georgiana asked, as she looked at the woman's swollen and cut hand.

'A footpad,' Mary said with a gasp of pain as Georgiana checked her arm, 'attacked that man.'

'But the policeman said you were on the other side of the Tank Stream, what were you doing there at this time of night?'

'I 'ad some business,' she said defiantly.

'Oh!' Georgiana said in a small voice, disappointed that Mary had obviously resorted to selling herself again.

'And it ain't what you're thinking, Duchess!'

Mary had several cuts on her fist where she'd punched the footpad and her arm was bruised where he'd hit her with his cudgel although fortunately nothing was broken. When Georgiana had bound up Mary's hand, Robert Croft, leader of the Foot Police patrol questioned her to find out what had happened.

Mary told him she'd taken a short cut

and when she'd seen someone charge out of the shadows towards a lone man, with a cudgel raised, she knew he was up to no good and she'd run forward and punched the attacker although she'd been too late to stop him hitting the man with a blow to the side of the head. She'd screamed, alerting two of Croft's men who'd been nearby and who'd apprehended the footpad, although not before he'd thrown her to the ground, where she'd fallen on her arm.

The attacker was well-known to the policemen.

'Andrew Patrick,' Croft said rolling his eyes upward, 'He can't seem to stop himself taking what ain't his. Wouldn't mind betting the judge decides he should hang this time,' he said cheerfully, 'Well, Miss,' he said to Mary, 'if you ever fancy a change of job, I'd have a place for someone like you in the Foot Police!'

'That wasn't exactly what happened, was it, Mary?' Georgiana said once the police had gone.

'No. But don't be angry, Duchess …'

'Why should I be angry? I don't understand.'

''E was followin' me down that alley.
So, it were my fault 'e got done over.'

'But who is he? And how do you know
him?'

Mary hung her head, 'I swear I did it
for you Duchess! I've been abandoned, I
know what it's like. I told 'im you'd died
and I thought he'd sail away and leave
you alone …'

'Who?' Georgiana asked softly, a
dreadful foreboding wrenching her
insides.

'The man … it's Lieutenant Brooks.'

Georgiana uttered a strangled cry. The
bowl of water she'd been using to wash
Mary's cuts, dropped to the ground and
smashed into pieces.

★ ★ ★

Georgiana sat next to Francis' bed
and studied his face. One side was so
swollen, his eye was merely a slit, the
other side was grazed where he'd hit the

269

ground and his hair was matted with blood. Surgeon Harrison had examined him and reported that other than bruising to his wrist which he'd presumably sustained when he fell, the only injury he'd received was to his head, although it wasn't possible to tell whether his eye had been damaged until the swelling subsided.

'I'll send another nurse to take over in a few hours, Duchess,' the doctor said.

But she told him she'd rather stay.

Francis lay motionless, unconscious and unaware she was there. She wanted to hold him or at least stroke his hand but she feared she'd hurt him. And anyway, she didn't trust herself to touch him. The emotional dam she'd constructed still held. She was on one side and on the other was love, disappointment, anguish and regret and all the other emotions she'd experienced. If the dam opened now, she'd be overwhelmed. And worse, she'd be open to more pain in the future. No, it was best if her emotions were kept strictly under control.

Why had he come looking for her? Perhaps he'd been aboard a ship which by chance had stopped in Sydney and while he was there, he thought he'd find her and see how she was for old times' sake?

It was possible Francis still believed he was her uncle. If Mama had died, she may have carried the secret of Georgiana's parentage to the grave.

But suppose he'd discovered the truth and he'd come to find her? Would they be able to rekindle their love or would they find they were now completely different people?

Or perhaps he wouldn't waken or recover from the blow to the head...

Georgiana pressed her palms to her temples and squeezed. There was no point asking herself so rnany questions. Francis was the only one who could answer most of them. The only question he couldn't answer was whether Georgiana would want to open the dam holding back her emotions and allow them all to rush out.

Francis began to come round several hours later. Surgeon Harrison tried to soothe Francis when, he realised he couldn't see anything, assuring him they'd do all they could to restore his sight, something that would be easier to determine once the swelling had subsided.

'Rest now, Lieutenant. Allow the injuries time to heal. A nurse will remain with you to attend to your needs.'

When the doctor had gone, Georgiana whispered, 'Francis? It's Georgiana. I'm here looking after you.'

He gasped and his hand reached out for hers.

'Georgiana, my love! Is it really you?' he asked and as she clasped his hand, he placed it against his lips, wincing with pain, yet still pressing it to his face. 'Thank God,' he said and she saw tears glisten in the lantern light as they squeezed between his eyelids and trickled down his cheeks, 'Touch me! Hold my hand! Anything to know you're really here. Somebody told me you'd died and I didn't believe them but I wasn't sure... I wasn't sure ... I feared ...' His voice cracked and he was unable to say more.

'Hush, Francis! I'm here now.'

'Georgiana, I need to tell you something important,' he said, his voice urgent and his breath coming in gasps, 'We're not blood-related. Our love wasn't tainted. We were free to be together!'

'Yes, I know. I received a letter from my mother, just days after you left Sydney.'

'Oh God, Georgiana! You found out just after I'd gone? How cruel!' His voice was thick with emotion, 'We could have been together all this time! Alice told me on my return to England and I immediately looked for a ship to come back to find you ...'

She wanted to cling to him, to envelop him in her arms to reassure him she was really there but she could do nothing more than hold his hand for fear of hurting him and because her own mind was reeling.

'Talk to me, Georgiana, tell me about your life. I long to see your face and I'm so afraid you'll disappear and I'll never be able to find you again. You won't leave me, will you?'

She kept hold of his hand while she told him about Dinah and Mary and her life as a nurse until she could hear the rhythm of his breathing deepen. It was good he was asleep. His body needed rest in order to recuperate.

He would recover, she told herself. There would be no lasting damage to his sight. Because Fate owed them some good fortune. It had dealt them blow after blow — in Francis' case, quite literally. Now, the balance had to be redressed. It doesn't work like that, Georgiana, a tiny voice inside her head whispered, Fate doesn't play by the rules.

★ ★ ★

'I thought she 'ad more pride,' Mary said with a snort, her lip curled in scorn.

'She deserves a bit o' happiness,' Dinah said.

'Yes, you're right, but he's not the one to give it to 'er. He's already left her once an' broken 'er heart.'

'She never said her heart was broken! You're just makin' that up!'

'What would you know? She never said anythin' but it was obvious to me.'

'Pish!' said Dinah, 'I think it's really romantic.'

'That's because yer head is stuffed with nonsense. Suppose 'e don't get his sight back? She'll spend the rest o' her days being his mother. There won't be any way she'll be able to become a doctor then.'

'Become a doctor? Duchess? Since when?'

'Couple o' days. She asked Surgeon White and he said yes.'

'How do you know?' Dinah's eyes narrowed with suspicion.

'Because she told me, but if she has to spend the rest o' her life lookin' after him ...'

'Well, I hear tell if it hadn't been for you, Lieutenant Brooks wouldn't be in that state. You never explained what you was doing on the other side o' Sydney that night walking down the same alley as Lieutenant Brooks ...'

'Never you mind!'

* * *

Time between Georgiana's shifts was spent with Francis, and although his bruises had faded, the grazes nearly healed and the swelling almost gone, his sight didn't return. During the day, or evening if the weather was fine, she led him outside with his arm tucked under hers to sit beneath a large tree. At night, she sat next to his bed, their heads close together.

He told her about the voyage back to England via China and how Captain Yeats had later admitted he'd deliberately embellished his account of Francis' behaviour at one of his dinners, to persuade his Naval Agent to stop drinking so heavily. When Francis spoke of life after he'd left her, his voice displayed an element of disbelief as if he were telling a story that had happened to someone else.

When Georgiana pictured him on the Lady Amelia among people she'd once known, the stories took on a reality which hurt, especially knowing he'd been drinking to excess and had been capable of doing something stupid like Captain Yeats had feared. Worse, speaking of that time reminded her with clarity, how she'd conditioned herself to deny her love. She hadn't intended to fall in love with him but when they'd first incorrectly believed they were related, she'd consciously destroyed that love, like a surgeon cutting away flesh. Now, although the memory of how she'd once felt about Francis remained and she felt tenderness towards him, she'd quashed her emotions so completely, she wondered if they would ever return.

At first, when they were together, Francis had spoken of how they would marry. How they would return to England where he'd give Georgiana the half of Cecile's estate which he'd inherited. He'd work tirelessly until her crimes had been pardoned and they'd live modestly together somewhere in the country. His words had been fervent at first but as the days passed and he remained blind, they became more wistful as if he were telling a fairy tale. And she became more doubtful it would happen. Worse, she'd finally realised the future of which Francis spoke wasn't what she wanted at all. She didn't want to return to England. And she didn't care about Cecile's will or money.

Before Francis had come, she'd been in control of her destiny. She didn't want the life he was offering her. But could she bear to see Francis leave? She knew she could not.

Georgiana had described some of the wonders of New South Wales but he seemed to have an aversion to Sydney — it had brought him nothing but grief. It was unlikely he'd want to spend the rest of his life there.

The more reserved she became, the more he withdrew into himself. Neither spoke to the other of their fears, although she knew his greatest fear was that he'd never regain his sight.

If that were so, then she'd give up everything to look after him. She owed him that, he'd lost his sight because he'd been searching for her. He'd made it clear he wanted to go back to England and planned to ask the governor for special dispensation to take her with him. If she was granted her freedom, she'd give up her opportunity to become a surgeon and she'd sail to England with him.

But something inside had begun to wither at the thought of giving up her dream.

Eventually, neither of them mentioned England and instead, they'd spoken about inconsequential matters. She'd described how she'd been horrified at being assigned to the same hut as Mary who she'd begun to win over by writing her letters and putting her name forward as a washerwoman.

'Although I don't think anyone can ever truly win Mary over!' Georgiana said, 'She's still as sharp-tongued to me as everyone else!'

'She's more a friend to you than you might realise,' Francis said, 'Despite her bluster and cursing. She tried to send me away after she'd told stories of you dying because she believed I'd hurt you unspeakably.'

'Not a happy outcome for you, though,' Georgiana said, stroking his face.

They were both silent for a while, each contemplating what life would be like if the blindness persisted.

Eventually Francis said, 'Dinah told me it was Mary who first called you Duchess.'

'Yes, she did it to mock me but later, she used it more kindly, like an affectionate nickname. And others picked it up.'

'It suits you,' Francis said, 'You have more dignity and gentility in your little finger than either of my sisters and their families, despite their pretensions at grandeur.'

She raised his fingers to her lips and kissed them.

'But how is it so many people in Sydney know you by that name?' Francis asked.

'I believe it was Arthur Towler's trial—' she said and stopped abruptly. She'd talked about her life in Sydney but there'd been two events she'd not mentioned — the incident with Towler and her friendship with David Oakley.

'Arthur Towler? Wasn't he the assistant carpenter aboard the Lady Amelia?'

'Yes,' she said brightly, 'but let's not talk about him.'

'What did he do? And why did people learn your name because of his trial?'

There was nothing for it, if Georgiana didn't tell him, she knew he'd ask Mary or Dinah and since it'd been revealed at the trial that he'd threatened her on the Lady Amelia, as well as other women, Francis would learn the entire story.

He was silent for some time after

she'd told him, staring sightlessly at the ground.

'So that's how you cut your finger with my razor when we were in Rio. Why didn't you tell me? I'd have protected you!' He finally said, his voice anguished.

'Because at the time, you were going to deliver me here and sail away. Later, when we fell in love, and planned to marry, there was no need to tell you because he wouldn't have touched me if you'd been here. And then when ...' she faltered, '... when I knew I'd be on my own and would have to take care of myself. I didn't want to antagonise him more than I'd already done.'

'So,' Francis said drawing a deep breath, 'The truth of the matter is that I failed completely to protect you ...' His voice broke with emotion and he buried his face in his hands.

'No, Francis! We had no choice in anything.'

He was silent and withdrawn when she led him back into the hospital.

As she helped him into bed, he said,

'I'm no use to you, and it seems I never have been.'

She clung to him and told him it wasn't true but he turned away from her.

* * *

The first face Francis wanted to see if his sight returned was Georgiana's.

It was, in fact, Dinah's.

When he woke, he was aware of shadows passing in front of him, then as the morning progressed, and with the utmost concentration, the shapes gained definition and colour. He held his hands up and tears came to his eyes as he strained to bring the hazy, pink shapes into focus.

'Lieutenant Brooks?' It was Dinah, who'd been passing his cot, 'Is something wrong?'

He turned his face to her, squinting and blinking rapidly, trying to force the blurry shapes to sharpen.

'You can see, can't you?' she said excitedly, 'Just wait until Duchess gets back, she'll be so relieved!'

'Where is she?'

'Out collecting berries.'

'Will she be back shortly?' Francis looked towards the entrance, practising focusing on distance as well as close up.

'I expect so ...' Dinah continued to linger, 'I 'ave an idea, Lieutenant. How about I take you outside? I know where she collects them berries...'

When Dinah spotted Georgiana, she was on her way back with a basketful of native currant berries but she'd stopped in the cemetery and was kneeling in front of David Oakley's grave.

'We'll just wait 'ere for Duchess, shall we? It looks like she's payin' her respects in the graveyard,' Dinah said.

Francis' vision had returned sufficiently for him to be able to make out a figure among white crosses, 'Who's buried there?' he asked, assuming it was a former patient.

'That's 'er fiancé's grave,' Dinah said, 'Surgeon Oakley. A real gentleman. Snake bite it was. Very sad.'

Francis blanched. There was so much

he didn't know about Georgiana, so much she'd been holding back. She hadn't intended to tell him about Arthur Towler and now, he'd discovered she'd been engaged to another. Why hadn't she told him that?

The time she'd spent in Sydney had certainly changed her.

'I expect it were Surgeon Oakley what gave 'er the idea of being a doctor,' Dinah said.

'A doctor?'

Dinah looked at him in surprise, 'Didn't she say to you, sir?'

He shook his head.

'Well, Surgeon White only told her a short while ago he'd allow it. I expect with you coming into hospital, she 'ad other things on 'er mind.'

'Dinah! Dinah!' Someone was calling impatiently from the direction of the hospital.

She looked back down the path nervously.

'I'll be all right on my own,' Francis said, 'I'll wait here for Georgiana. You go back.'

Dinah nodded gratefully and when her name was called again with more urgency, she turned and hurried along the path to the hospital.

Georgiana looked up as the exasperated cries for Dinah grew louder and she saw Francis watching her from the edge of the cemetery with his hand to his face, shielding his eyes from the sunlight. His appearance there could only mean one thing and picking up the basket of berries, she rushed towards him.

'Your sight's returned?'

His eyes, unused to such brightness, were streaming with tears but he nodded and she rushed into his arms.

'That's such marvellous news! But what was Dinah thinking in bringing you out so soon? And then to leave you here ...'

'Don't be angry with her. She knew I was desperate to tell you. And this short walk has been so enlightening ... May I offer you my condolences on the loss of your fiancé.'

She stepped back and saw his pained expression. 'Francis ... I ... '

'And of course, my congratulations on your new position in the hospital.'

'Francis, I can explain'

'Georgiana, there's no need. You owe me nothing. You've never asked me for anything. It seems throughout your life you've been a pawn in other people's games, doing whatever suited them. It's time for you to do something for yourself. I only wish I'd realised that sooner. I came back here because I wanted to be with you and to take you home with me. I was arrogant and thoughtless. I didn't want to believe you'd find someone else to love or that you'd want to stay here.'

'But Francis'

He held his finger to her lips to silence her, 'Everything's changed, Georgiana. I didn't want to acknowledge it but having regained my sight, now it's obvious. You don't feel the same way anymore, I thought I could hear it in your voice but now I can see it in your eyes for myself.

'And why should you feel the same?

Your life's moved on. As soon as the Peregrine leaves, I shall be aboard. You have your own life to live.'

She caught hold of his arm as he turned away but when she saw Surgeon Harrison striding angrily towards them, she let go.

'Lieutenant Brooks! I've reprimanded that foolish nurse most severely! You should not be out here in the strong sunlight. Come! Too much brightness is not good.'

Georgiana watched the two men walk away with a heavy weight in her chest.

She wanted to love Francis again as she had done before, though that felt like a lifetime ago.

She was sure she could love him again. So why did she feel like stone inside?

* * *

Georgiana's shift had finished and she decided to go for a walk before returning home to sleep. She headed towards the observatory near the western point.

It'd be unlikely she'd encounter anyone and she'd have a chance to sort out her thoughts alone.

As she flanked the woods, the hair stood up on the back of her neck and she had the eerie feeling someone was watching her although she could see no one. Then a few yards ahead, a dark figure stepped silently out of the undergrowth, a spear in his hand. His gaze transfixed her and as he raised the weapon, she held her breath waiting for the blow but it was merely a signal, because a woman slipped out of the shadows and following her, was a small boy. The trio stared silently at Georgiana, then taking the boy's hand, the woman stepped forward and untying a net bag from around her waist, she crouched and placed it at Georgiana's feet.

As she looked up, Georgiana recognised her. It was the mother who'd brought the young boy inlo the hospital when he'd been suffering from smallpox. The woman emptied the contents of the bag on the ground and stood up. Still she said nothing, just looked down at her son and ruffled his curly hair, then stared directly into Georgiana's eyes, holding her gaze while a silent, mystical interchange took place between the two women.

Finally, mother and son walked back to the man, and picking the boy up, the woman rested him on her hip, and in a few steps, had melted into the forest. Like a wisp of smoke blown by the wind, the man was gone too.

Georgiana stooped to pick up the items the woman had left. There was a duck, two fishes and an oyster shell which the natives used for sharpening spears. They were gifts. No words had been spoken but she'd seen the way the mother had looked at her son, then up at Georgiana as if to show her gratitude. When they'd turned back to the father, Georgiana had seen the love in his eyes and briefly, he'd gazed at her as if to say thank you. Again, the hairs stood up on the back of her neck but this time, not in fear but with raw emotion.

The silent exchange had been something remarkable. How wonderful to witness such love and devotion. And such a thoughtful gift of food which, it was obvious from their skinny bodies, they could ill afford. Georgiana could scarcely draw breath for the emotions which bubbled up inside and continued to flow. Sobs wracked her body and she remained kneeling on the ground until she had no more tears.

She was exhausted, yet exhilarated as if in this untamed landscape with its enormous skies and endless horizons, she'd witnessed pure love and it had allowed her to be reborn.

9

One year later, Georgiana had served more than half her sentence; and although still a convict, most people treated her with respect not usually shown to the prisoners. She owned a new, sturdy, brick-built house surrounded by acres of land and was still training to be a doctor with Surgeon White and his team. However, many people sought her help and medical advice rather than consult her colleagues. The natives especially, often found their way to her house to ask for help, knowing they'd receive a warmer welcome from her than from many other colonists.

Now, she sat on her shady veranda watching two servants, far off, working in her fields. As far as the eye could see, the land belonged to her although she considered she was merely borrowing it from the people who'd been there before her, the Aborigines, and she'd given instructions to her servants to allow the natives to take what they believed was theirs. Food was always available at her kitchen for visitors, whoever they were.

A storm was coming. In the distance, Silhouetted against the steely thunder. clouds that gathered behind the ridge, three tiny figures holding spears walked in single file. Off hunting, she supposed. As she'd done many times before, she remembered the day the Aborigine family had come to find her and thank her.

No words had been exchanged and yet, she'd glimpsed their deep, abiding love for each other. There'd been nothing complicated about the family. The bonds which bound them were primeval and natural and she'd been transported to a time before her father had left, when love had been spontaneous and joyful, and not something to suppress. Inside her, the dam she'd constructed had burst and she'd felt an upsurge of emotion which seemed to lift her from the ground as if she were floating. Georgiana had stumbled back to the hospital, her senses reeling at the heightened intensity of everything around her — the muted grey-greens of the foliage was now vivid; the scent of the Eucalyptus sharper and tangier and the birdsong louder and purer.

She wondered if they were truly her emotions, the ones she'd denied for so long. And if so, would they last or simply bubble up and be lost? She'd become accustomed to feeling cold inside, but now she burned with a heat that was frightening. But suppose when she saw Francis, she felt nothing, just the memories of passion?

Georgiana had hesitated at the door of the hospital, not sure if she wanted to find out but Mary, with an armful of blankets had come up behind her and shoved her, 'Well, don't stand there like a lump, Duchess, hold the door open!'

When she did, Georgiana couldn't resist glancing towards Francis' bed, where Surgeon Harrison was examining his eyes. She'd gasped at the rush of love she felt for Francis when she saw his face, even surpassing the feelings she'd had for him on the Lady Amelia, as if they'd been silently strengthening on the other side of the dam, and suddenly broken through.

'Something's changed,' Francis had said as soon as the doctor left them alone, 'I can hear it in your voice. And your eyes are different ... You must have loved your fiancé very much for a visit to his grave to touch you so deeply ...'

She'd shaken her head, 'No, Francis, I never loved David. If you can see love in my eyes, it's all for you. Something extraordinary just happened to me ...' Her words tripped over themselves as she'd rushed to tell him about her encounter with the natives. 'Do you still love me?' she asked.

'Till the end of my days!' he'd said, taking her hands, 'So, what does this mean? Do you want still to marry me?'

'Yes! Oh, yes! I want to be with you always!'

'Then let's marry as soon as possible and stay in Sydney so you can carry on with your studies.'

'But don't you want to go home?'

'My home is wherever you are,' Francis said.

She flung her arms around his neck.

'The sooner we marry the better,' he said, 'We've been kept apart too long already.'

★   ★   ★

Dinah, Mary and the other nurses organised the wedding and on the day Francis left hospital, he and Georgiana were married by Reverend Leston in the presence of the hospital staff, captain and officers of the Peregrine and assorted people from Sydney and beyond. How strange she'd married into the family which she'd once believed was her own! She had a new surname — Brooks — but no one in Sydney cared about the Brooks or the Tilcotts, most people still referred to Georgiana as Duchess.

Until Francis' finances could be transferred to Sydney, including Cecile's legacy which he intended to give to Georgiana, he bought a small, sandstone house on the eastern side of Sydney where the couple went after their wedding.

As soon as they were alone, Francis drew Georgiana to him and held her tightly. She'd hardly dared believe they were at last together and she was overtaken with shyness and hesitation. Consistently, Fate had ripped them apart and now neither of them could conceive they were finally together.

'If we're quiet,' she whispered, 'Fate might not notice us ...'

As she spoke, there was a peal of thunder in the distance and raindrops began to drum on the roof, lazily at first and then more insistently as a streak of lightning flashed across the sky.

'The storm's coming this way,' he said, nuzzling her neck, 'and it might just keep Fate distracted while we ...'

He slipped his hand behind her back and, lifting her in his arms, he carried her to the bedroom and laid her on the bed. Slowly, he undressed her, beginning with her shoes and stockings and as he revealed the creamy skin of each part of her body, he kissed and caressed it before removing the next item of clothing until they lay naked together while the storm raged outside, hiding the sound of their love-making, and fuelling their desire and passion.

* * *

The thud of hooves brought Georgiana back to the present and she ran down the steps to meet her husband. Francis swung out of the saddle and walked quickly towards her as a servant led his horse away. He enveloped her in his arms as if they'd been apart for days, not hours.

When Cecile's money had arrived, Francis had given it to Georgiana and she'd bought them the house with the veranda and acres of land which Francis was cultivating with the help of their convict servants. The soil was good and they were taming the wild countryside and prospering. At last, Fate seemed to be smiling upon them.

'The storm's coming, Duchess,' Francis whispered with a slow smile and her heart skipped a beat, 'There'll be no more work in the fields until it's passed,' he said, and slipping his arm behind her back, he lifted her and carried her to their bedroom.

As their kisses became more urgent, their bodies melted together as if they were two halves of one whole. Outside, heavy clouds rolled over Sydney and lightning crackled its zig-zag course across the sky closely followed by roaring claps of thunder which shook the earth. Somewhere in the woods, a flash of electricity ignited a eucalyptus tree which flared brightly, showering the earth with sparks.

Later, when the storm had passed and their passion spent, Georgiana lay in Francis' arms, delighting in their closeness with her cheek against his shoulder and her arm across his chest, rising and falling with each breath.

On the other side of the world in a country which considered itself civilised, her life had been of such low value, she'd been sacrificed to save her selfish cousin, Margaret. She'd been banished to the furthest reaches of the globe in punishment.

Yet here in this land of raw beauty and primeval magic, she'd found the most precious thing it was possible to give and to possess ... true love.

We do hope that you have enjoyed reading this large print book.

Did you know that all of our titles are available for purchase?

We publish a wide range of high quality large print books including:
Romances, Mysteries, Classics
General Fiction
Non Fiction and Westerns

Special interest titles available in large print are:
The Little Oxford Dictionary
Music Book, Song Book
Hymn Book, Service Book

Also available from us courtesy of Oxford University Press:
Young Readers' Dictionary
(large print edition)
Young Readers' Thesaurus
(large print edition)

For further information or a free brochure, please contact us at:
Ulverscroft Large Print Books Ltd.,
The Green, Bradgate Road, Anstey,
Leicester, LE7 7FU, England.
Tel: (00 44) **0116 236 4325**
Fax: (00 44) **0116 234 0205**

THE LOVE TREE

Patricia Keyson

When Lily arrives at The Limes to work as a maid for two sisters, Eta and Mabel, little does she know she will instantly fall in love with their handsome lodger, Samuel. When Cecil Potts visits the sisters' beer house and shop, a tale of murder, death and deceit unravels. Will Lily and Samuel ever step out from Cecil's dark shadow to find happiness under the love tree?

ANNIE'S CASTLE BY THE SEA

Christina Garbutt

After a lifetime of putting her daughter first, widowed Annie travels to the beautiful Italian island of Vescovina for a summer. Annie's soon swept up in the magic of the place, but when the town is under threat by developers it's up to Annie and her gorgeous new friend, Giovanni, to save it. But as pressure begins to mount, is it really the town that needs saving – or Annie's heart?

GREEN SKIES AT NIGHT

Alan C. Williams

When a wide-ranging Green Skies weather phenomenon threatens the people of Tulsa, Oklahoma with destruction, it's up to meteorologist Amber Devane to warn them. The trouble is, the local media don't believe her predictions. She must put aside her recovery from an operation to save her family and her county. Aided by school-friend Ryan, a native American astronomer, the two of them must fight the tumultuous weather and prejudices as well as struggle with their own whirlwind budding romance …

PENNY WISE

Ewan Smith

Penny can't wait to go on the holiday of a lifetime with her best friend, Angela. But then comes some terrible news: her father has had a heart-attack. Now she will have to spend the summer looking after her parents' little seaside shop instead. That wouldn't be so bad but the neighbouring LoPrice supermarket has its eyes on the property. And Penny isn't sure what to make of the assistant manager, Graham Fraser. He's young, good-looking — and very ambitious.

BEYOND HER DREAMS

Gail Richards

England, 1848. Housemaid Alice is taken from the big house she works in to be the only servant to Mrs Younger. The first person she meets is Daniel, whose friendly face she remembers in the dark, lonely days that follow. She dreams of romance but Daniel has a sweetheart — hasn't he? Then Mrs Younger disappears and it's up to Alice to find her. Will Daniel help or is he too interested in someone else?

A SUITABLE COMPANION

Philippa Carey

Earl Barton's daughter's new governess is collected from the stagecoach stop. However, the next morning they discover Clara Thompson is the wrong young lady — she had been expecting to be companion to a Lady Sutton. But Lady Sutton refuses to exchange her for the intended governess! They have to keep Clara on to help them with the tantrum-prone young Lady Mary while they find a replacement governess. However, could it be that the wrong young lady turns out to be the earl's right young lady?